A Baby for the Deputy

CATHY McDAVID

MILLS
BOON

First Published in Great Britain 2017
By Mills & Boon, an imprint of HarperCollins*Publishers*
1 London Bridge Street, London, SE1 9GF

Large Print edition 2017

© 2017 Cathy McDavid

ISBN: 978-0-263-07181-8

Printed and bound in Great Britain
by CPI Antony Rowe, Chippenham, Wiltshire

Aaron lifted her off her feet and hard against him.

"Is this a good idea?" Mel's voice wavered. The message earlier had been hands-off.

"You can tell me no." He lowered his mouth, stopping a millimeter shy of kissing her. "Otherwise, hang on."

Hang on? Like to his shoulders? Weak in the knees, she decided maybe she'd better. Just as a precaution.

In the deepest recesses of her mind, a small voice shouted a warning to be careful. This was inviting danger.

She didn't listen. Aaron smelled too delicious and felt too good for her to stop now.

"I've missed you, Mel." He brushed his lips across hers, the touch softer than a butterfly's wings.

The words she'd longed to hear. Aaron had never said them before, in this or any context. Missing her implied he thought about her when they were apart. Hadn't she just ripped the rug out from under him with her pregnancy announcement? Yet, he admitted to missing her.

This wasn't just a matter of growing feelings. There had to be more.

Since 2006, *New York Times* bestselling author **Cathy McDavid** has been happily penning contemporary Westerns for Mills & Boon. Every day, she gets to write about handsome cowboys riding the range or busting a bronc. It's a tough job, but she's willing to make the sacrifice. Cathy shares her Arizona home with her own real-life sweetheart and a trio of odd pets. Her grown twins have left to embark on lives of their own, and she couldn't be prouder of their accomplishments.

To the lovely and dedicated members of Cathy's Crew–thanks for being part of my street team and helping me get the word out. You're the best!

Chapter One

Sensing danger, Melody Hartman quickly straightened and scrambled out of the way. A split second later, the horse's rear hoof sliced the air in the exact spot where Mel's head had just been.

She pretended to wipe sweat from her brow. "Whew. That was close."

"Sorry." The horse's owner, a tall, trim woman in her fifties, tugged on the bay's halter. "This fellow has a temper. I should have warned you."

"It's okay." Mel relaxed her grip on the surgical scissors she held and let out a sigh, grateful her instincts had once again paid off. "Not my first near miss."

The truth was, Mel encountered far closer calls on a regular basis. As recently as this morning, she'd been knocked to the ground by a potbellied pig, narrowly missing the steely prongs of a pitchfork. Last week, she'd been stomped on by an eighteen-hundred-pound bull, miraculously escaping with only minor cuts and contusions. An infected cat scratch recently sent her to the emergency medical clinic.

Such was the daily life of Mustang Valley's sole resident veterinarian. Dangers and difficulties aside, she wouldn't trade her job for the world. Mel was living her dream. Quite literally. She'd wanted to be a veterinarian for as long as she could remember, and buying Doc Palmer's practice when he retired a few months ago had turned that dream into reality.

"Think you should give him more tranquilizers?" the woman asked, shielding her eyes from the glaring Arizona sun.

They were at Powell Ranch, the largest and

oldest horse operation in the area. The woman was one of many people who boarded their horses there and made use of the riding facilities.

Mel shook her head. "I don't want him so sleepy he lays down on us. The wound's right between his gaskin and stifle. He could pull on the flesh and inflict more damage."

The bay was tied to a post at the far end of the outdoor stalls. He'd gotten into a scuffle with his neighbor, a shaggy and even more temperamental pony, who'd retaliated by biting the bay and leaving two gaping holes on his left rear leg. Unfortunately, the injury went unnoticed for a couple of days—the horse's owner had been out of town. By the time she discovered the wound, it was inflamed, infected and just plain nasty.

Seeing the bay's eyes drift close, Mel decided to make another attempt at removing the necrotic tissue. The procedure didn't hurt the horse. He'd kicked at Mel more out of anger than pain. Also, just like some people, he wasn't a good patient.

"Hold him steady," Mel told the woman as she quickly snipped away with the scissors. Finishing that task, she cleansed the wound again and applied a liberal glob of medicated ointment.

"Are you going to stitch him up?" the woman asked, peering around the bay's head.

Mel continued to assess the wound. "I don't think so. The edges are too ragged for sutures to hold. Better we stick to a strict antibiotic regiment. You know how to give injections?"

"Me? I'm an old pro."

Many livestock owners, especially those in rural areas, were capable of doctoring their animals to some degree. Vets were consulted for only the more serious cases.

"Good. I'll leave you enough penicillin and syringes for two weeks. He's going to need twice daily injections." Mel ran her hand gingerly down the bay's leg. "No sense bandaging the wound, either. It won't hold."

"He'd just chew it off," the woman said with a resigned sigh.

Mel started to pack her case. Before closing it,

she handed the woman her jar of salve. "Cleanse the wound at the same time you give him the injections and apply this. Call me if he's not showing any improvement or the wound becomes reinfected."

"Thanks for coming out on such short notice."

"No problem."

Mel carried her case to her truck while the woman returned the sleepy horse to his stall. Setting the case on the ground, she leaned against the hood and stifled a yawn. The bay wasn't the only one who was tired. Mel had been up and hard at it since five this morning, nearly nine hours ago, with no break.

As she opened the storage compartment on her truck, she was struck with a sudden wave of nausea and light-headedness. Hugging her middle, she waited for the sensation to pass, hoping she hadn't caught that flu bug going around.

Tomorrow was a big day. She, her two sisters and her new stepmom were throwing a huge sixtieth birthday party for her dad at the Cowboy Up Café where her older sister worked.

They still had a lot to do, and the last thing Mel needed was to be under the weather.

Fortunately, the nausea passed, and the next instant, Mel felt perfectly fine. That was... strange.

She might have thought more about it if not for a black SUV turning the corner of the horse barn, distracting her. The writing and logo emblazoned on each side identified the vehicle as belonging to the Maricopa County Sheriff's Department. Three deputies were assigned to Mustang Valley and its nearest neighbor, Rio Verde. They were often spotted patrolling the streets, parked in front of people's homes or, like today, at one of the ranches.

The driver's door opened, and a pair of familiar leather cowboy boots hit the ground, followed by long legs clad in dark brown slacks and a khaki uniform shirt. Mel's heart gave a flutter as it always did upon seeing this particular deputy, and she promptly forgot all about stowing her case.

As she watched, he walked slowly, yet deliberately, toward her. She imagined a twinkle in the vivid blue eyes he hid behind aviator sunglasses. Recalled how the bristles of his five-o'clock shadow tickled her palm when she cradled his cheek.

"Dr. Hartman." He nodded in greeting.

Pushing aside her long braid, a silly, nervous habit she wished she could break, she smiled with more reservation than if they were alone. "Afternoon, Deputy Travers."

"Is Ethan nearby? I was told I might find him with you."

"Actually, he's over there." She indicated the row of outdoor stalls. "At least, he was earlier."

"Thanks." He tugged on the brim of his felt cowboy hat, hesitated briefly and then continued on.

A stranger might not realize they were well acquainted, and, to be honest, they preferred it that way. For the last year and a half, Aaron Travers and his family had lived in Mustang Valley, moving here when he transferred from the Phoenix Police Department. He and Mel occasionally ran into each other, as everyone ran into one another sooner or later in a small town.

There were also those encounters that weren't accidental. But she and Aaron didn't talk about them. Not with anyone else.

Once he'd passed and her heart rate slowed, she returned to stowing her supplies. The sensation of awareness he'd left in his wake wound through her, interfering with her ability to concentrate.

Bam! Another wave of nausea hit Mel, and she swallowed, willing her queasy stomach to settle. By some miracle, it did. A moment later she was fine, as if she hadn't been nauseous at all.

She'd just finished preparing her invoice for the horse owner when Ethan Powell and Aaron— make that Deputy Travers—approached.

"Mel," Ethan said, "do you have a minute? Aaron has some questions for you."

"Sure." She set down her invoice pad. "How can I help, Deputy?"

"Last night, three horses went missing from the Sanford place."

Mel drew back in alarm. "You're kidding!"

"It's the third incident this month," Aaron said. "I'm pretty sure we're dealing with rustlers."

"I can't believe it."

The first missing horses had been considered a fluke. A few even claimed they'd escaped their pasture and joined a wild herd often spotted near the Salt River. Then, after a second group of horses disappeared, people took notice. But horse rustling? That seemed like something out of the Old West. Not modern day.

"Why?" she asked, still grappling with the news. "None of the horses were particularly valuable. Mostly ranch stock."

"Slaughter?"

Mel's off-and-on sensitive stomach gave a lurch. She regularly dealt with the death of animals, many of the circumstances heartbreaking. As a result, she'd learned to cope. Still, the idea of horses being stolen for the purpose of profiting from their slaughter sickened her.

"Aaron's visiting all the area ranch owners," Ethan said. "Seeing if they've noticed anything suspicious in recent months and asking them to check with their employees."

"What can I do?" Mel asked Aaron.

"You travel the valley on a regular basis," he said. "Just keep your eyes and ears open. Contact the station if you spot anything out of the ordinary. Unfamiliar vehicles parked where they don't belong. Strangers lingering or asking unusual questions. Don't worry that you're being overly paranoid."

"Of course," Mel said. "Absolutely."

"I appreciate it."

After another nod, he and Ethan wandered a short distance away, continuing their conversation. Mel studied them before returning to her invoice. She'd give it to the horse owner on her way out. After checking her schedule, she phoned her next customer and gave him a heads-up on her impending arrival.

She was about to climb into the truck when Aaron unexpectedly appeared in her peripheral vision. She turned, her hand resting on the door. "Hi."

"Are you okay?"

"I'm fine. Why?" She automatically glanced about to see if they were being observed. Another nervous habit.

"You look pale."

"Do I?" Mel touched her face, only to let her hand drop. "I got up early. And," she added, suddenly recalling, "I missed lunch."

"You work too hard."

It was true. She did. But she had no choice. Not if she expected to make her monthly payments to Doc Palmer.

"Speaking of which, I'd better go. I have another appointment." She smiled, wished for just a moment they were alone and started to slide in behind the steering wheel. She didn't suggest calling him later. Chitchatting on the phone wasn't something they did.

Aaron's next words stopped her. "See you to-morrow. At the party."

"You're going?" That was a surprise. Mel had reviewed the guest list last night and knew his name wasn't on it.

"Dolores invited us. She and Nancy are in the same Bunko group."

"Right. I forgot."

"You don't mind?"

Mel dismissed his concerns with a nonchalant wave. "Dad'll be glad to have you there. All of you."

By all of you, Mel meant Aaron's almost three-year-old daughter and his mother-in-law, Nancy, who'd lived with him and his daughter since the death of Aaron's wife.

Granted, their arrangement might seem a bit unconventional to some, but apparently it worked. Nancy's late daughter had been her only child. Watching her granddaughter during the day, sharing Aaron's home, allowed her to stay connected while also providing him with a trustworthy and devoted caregiver. At least, that was how he'd explained it to Mel.

All at once, Ethan returned from wherever it was he'd gone and hailed Aaron.

"Go on," Mel told him, and hopped in her truck. "I'm running late as it is."

"Do me a favor. Eat and get some rest." Before she could start the ignition, he placed a hand on her shoulder and squeezed gently.

She wanted to be mad. He was breaking their strictest rule. Except it was hard to be mad when her shoulder tingled deliciously at his touch and continued to even after he'd moved off.

Mel shut the truck door and drove away, almost forgetting to drop off her invoice with the horse owner on her way out.

Reaching the end of the long drive leading down the mountain from the ranch, she stopped and let the truck idle. Since she and Aaron had begun seeing each other, they'd both worried how people, like Nancy for instance, might be hurt. It was yet another reason for the two of them to keep their relationship casual and private.

Lately, however, Mel worried about her vulnerable heart. She hadn't counted on her feelings for Aaron growing and did her best to hide it from him.

She let out a long sigh. What had seemed so simple at first was slowly becoming complicated. Aaron and his family attending her father's party, and his mother-in-law developing a friendship with Mel's stepmom certainly wasn't helping matters. Neither was her upset stomach, which gave another lurch.

Nerves. And stress. Those had to be the reasons. Mel refused to consider anything else.

AARON WAS MAKING his third trip of the day to the Sanford place. The first time he'd arrived at 6:20 a.m. in response to the 9-1-1 call. He'd returned at 9:50 a.m. when Ken Sanford, Sr. called to say he'd discovered fresh tire tracks behind their far pasture—no one had driven the dirt road since before the last rains.

Now, Aaron was heading to the ranch for another look around, planning to focus on the cut fence where the thieves had entered the property. When his cop's gut told him to persist, he usually did. There was always the chance he'd missed something during his previous inspections.

Horse rustling. Who'd have guessed he'd be investigating a crime of that nature in this day and age? A search of records at the station revealed the last such incident committed in Mustang Valley had been in the 1930s. Wow.

Aaron observed every detail as he drove, despite frequently traveling this road. He couldn't help himself—too many years on the force. That didn't stop the other half of his brain from wandering. Specifically to Mel. Not that he didn't always think of her when they weren't together.

She'd looked unwell earlier, and that bothered him. He understood the lines of fatigue on her pretty oval face. With her demanding schedule, that wasn't uncommon. Rather, it was the lack of color in her cheeks and slowness of her steps concerning him.

She was almost always happy and vivacious— a ball of energy contained inside a petite package. Those qualities more than her sparkling brown eyes and curvy figure were what caused him to notice her two winters ago at the community's Holly Daze Festival.

After that, it was hard not to keep noticing her and, eventually, talk to her. Just being in her proximity breathed new life into parts of Aaron's heart and soul he'd thought forever darkened.

Dangerous feelings and ones he shouldn't have. Not if he wanted the life he'd scraped together for him and his daughter, Kaylee, to remain calm, quiet and stable. Emphasis on the last word. That was why he'd quit the Phoenix Police Department and taken the less demanding job of deputy sheriff.

His phone abruptly rang. The personal one he kept in his vehicle, strictly for family and close friends. Snatching it from the cubby, he glimpsed his sister's name and photo on the display. The picture of her and Kaylee was one of his favorites, taken during his sister's last visit.

"Hey, Pickle."

She groaned expansively. No secret, she hated the childhood nickname. Which was why Aaron insisted on using it.

"What's up?" he asked.

"Bad time to call?"

Hearing Joanna's voice immediately thrust him back in time to their family's rural home in Queen Creek and their life together growing up. She'd moved to Seattle a year ago, and he missed her terribly. She'd been his rock, his staunchest supporter and his sounding board during the many difficult months Aaron's wife was ill and every day since she'd died.

"I'm on the road," he said. "Have about ten minutes."

"Don't tell me." Joanna laughed, the sound rich and vibrant. "A rancher let his hound dog run loose, and it got in with the lady down the street's King Charles spaniel."

He pretended to be affronted. "Believe it or not, there's real crime in Mustang Valley."

"Riiiiiight." She drew the single word out over three syllables.

"We've had a recent rash of horse thefts."

"No fooling? That actually sounds serious."

"I'm on my way now to talk to the third victim."

"Do you have any leads?"

"Not yet. I've been interviewing the locals." Most people didn't realize that 90 percent of good detective work was questioning potential witnesses.

"Locals like Mel?"

Aaron paused, not wanting to give his sister any ideas. "She's a regular at most of the ranches in the valley and might run across something."

"How you two doing?"

"We're not dating."

"Hey, hey," Joanna protested. "Don't get mad.

I think what you and Mel have is great. More couples should be as open-minded as you two."

"Yeah." Except, what Aaron and Mel had didn't feel open-minded to him.

"Something wrong?" Joanna asked.

"I don't know." He blew out a long breath. "Lately, I've been thinking she deserves more than casual hookups."

"Did she say so?"

"No."

"Are *you* tired of the arrangement?"

"Yes, but not in the way you think."

Joanna gave a delighted gasp. "You love her."

He gave a start and steadied his free hand on the steering wheel. "I wouldn't say that." Not yet, anyway. "I like her. A lot."

"Well, you should like the person you're sleeping with."

"Am I being a jerk? Taking her for granted?" It was the opinion he'd recently formed of himself.

"Come on. You and Mel have an arrangement. A good, sensible arrangement that works. Nei-

ther of you are ready or in a position for all
the demands of a committed relationship. Yet,
you're human, and human beings require intimacy. You and she have come up with a cre-
ative solution. You get together a couple times
a month for a few discreet hours of adult pleasure. No strings attached. It's perfect."

"Spoken like a psychology major."

"Spoken like a feminist," she said, correcting
him. "I wish I could find someone with your
progressive attitude. Beats being single."

His sister was the only person Aaron had told
about his and Mel's secret arrangement, and
there were days he wished he hadn't.

Cripes, what was wrong with him? There was
nothing sordid or dirty or wrong about what he
and Mel did. She was completely on board. In
fact, she'd been the one to originally suggest it.
Yes, in a roundabout way, but not so subtle that
Aaron hadn't understood and, after a long, emotional tug-of-war with himself, agreed.

She was beautiful and smart and as sexy as

hell. When they were alone, she displayed the kind of passion he'd always hoped to find in a woman. Which only increased the guilt eating away at him. He could and did tell himself he wasn't being disloyal to Robin. She'd been gone nearly three years.

His heart argued differently, insisting he was dishonoring his late wife's memory. Aaron's mother-in-law would agree.

"Mel should be with a guy who can offer her more," he said to Joanna. "A guy who's emotionally free."

"If that was what she wanted, she'd give you the boot."

"Sometimes, I wish she would." Then he could stop wanting what he couldn't have and beating himself up over it.

"You're worried about Nancy," Joanna said, "and you shouldn't be."

"If she ever found out—"

"What? She'd leave? Go home to Ohio?"

"I don't want that. She loves Kaylee, and Kaylee loves her."

"If Nancy left, that would be her choice and her mistake to make."

Aaron rubbed his suddenly throbbing forehead. His arrangement with Mel was supposed to be without strings and without angst, yet it wasn't. In hindsight, they'd been silly and stupid.

He had, anyway. Truthfully, Aaron wasn't entirely sure how Mel felt about him. She didn't talk about it. Ever. And she didn't encourage him to, either.

"You're single," Joanna continued. "It's not fair that Nancy expects you to remain that way for the rest of your life."

"Isn't it?"

"You aren't betraying Robin."

"I made a promise to her," he bit out.

"To never fall in love again?"

"To devote myself to Kaylee. I owe Robin that much. She gave up her life for our daughter."

Joanna's voice softened. "You couldn't save

her, Aaron. No one could. At best, she might have lived a few more months. And you probably wouldn't have had Kaylee. A lot of people, me included, think she made the right decision."

That didn't lessen his loss, relieve his guilt or diminish his hurt.

A few weeks after learning she was pregnant, Robin began having severe headaches that over-the-counter pain relievers wouldn't touch. Two weeks later, she was seeing a specialist and undergoing all manner of tests. Aaron would never forget sitting in the doctor's office and hearing the diagnosis: inoperable brain tumor. And then hearing the prognosis: terminal.

Robin refused any treatment that might have extended her life because it would harm the baby. At thirty-four weeks pregnant, she'd delivered a small but healthy baby girl. Unfortunately, it was too late for her. The treatments she'd previously refused had no effect on her rapidly growing tumor, and she lost the battle when Kaylee was just a few weeks old.

Robin's wish to be a mother had been fulfilled

and, in the process, she'd given Aaron a last precious gift. He would do nothing to jeopardize Kaylee's safety and happiness.

"Why don't you talk to Mel," Joanna suggested. "If you're having doubts."

"Or, I could just end things."

"You could. Except that isn't what you want."

Should he tell his sister what he really wanted was to date Mel and not just sleep with her? No, Joanna would have a field day with that one, and Aaron wasn't in the mood.

"Pickle, can I call you later? I'm almost at my next stop." Not entirely a lie; the Sanfords were less than a mile down the road.

"Tomorrow. I've got plans later," she added with a teasing tone.

"Have fun."

"Oh, I intend to." She laughed again.

Aaron disconnected, his thoughts a jumble. He really did like Mel and hated the thought of ending things. But he was being grossly unfair to her. She may think she preferred whatever this was they had, but deep down, she was a forever and ever kind of gal. Aaron wasn't fooled for one minute.

A quarter mile up the road, he spied an older model pickup and rusty horse trailer pulled off to the south side of the road. The truck hood was up, signaling trouble, and someone sat in the driver's seat.

He slowed, determining the driver to be a young woman. As he passed, she rolled down her window and waved at him. Aaron executed a swift U-turn and parked behind the trailer. A reddish-brown tail hung out over the rear gate and swished aimlessly.

Before getting out, he radioed the station, then proceeded with caution all the while making mental notes. The situation didn't appear dangerous, but he took nothing for granted.

Nearing the driver's door, he realized the young woman was on the phone.

"Good afternoon." He looked her over. "Having some trouble?"

"I broke down. The engine light came on and

then smoke started coming out from under the hood."

"License and registration, please."

"Have I done something wrong?" Her voice quavered.

"Just routine."

Producing the required documents, she passed them through the open window, still clutching her phone. Aaron decided she must have maintained an open line as a precaution. Smart move. She wasn't very old, maybe not even out of high school, and pretty, even with her torn jeans, faded tank top and ratty old ball cap. Add to that her disabled vehicle, and she was a potential sitting duck.

Aaron reviewed the documents, noting the eighteen-year-old's name and home address of Flagstaff. He compared her face to the tiny picture. Something about her struck a familiar chord, but he couldn't quite put his finger on it.

"Be right back." In his vehicle, he ran her name and license plate. Nothing significant came back. What had he expected?

Returning to her truck, he handed over the documents. "You're a long ways from home."

"I'm staying with my...with friends in Mustang Valley."

"Are they on their way to help you?"

"Uh...no. I wasn't able to reach them."

"I see." Aaron suspected she was coloring the truth and didn't know why. "Do you have a roadside assistance service?"

"I don't think so."

"What about your parents?"

"My mom can't help."

"Because she's in Flagstaff," Aaron stated.

"Yeah. And at work. I'm not supposed to call her unless it's an emergency."

"This might qualify."

The girl, Samantha, according to her driver's license, shook her head. "I'm not calling. She's busy."

"And your friends aren't available?"

In response, her mouth firmed to a thin line.

There was definitely more going on than she was telling him, and he didn't trust her. Nonetheless, she'd broken no laws and was in distress. Not to mention her truck and trailer were a potential hazard and the horse would need water soon. Aaron had a duty to help her.

"Sit tight," he said, and walked to the front of the truck where he inspected the engine. Heat wafted off in waves, and it made a soft hissing sound. The smoke she'd claimed to see was probably steam.

A moment later, she disobeyed his order and joined him, anxiously watching as if he might sabotage the engine rather than repair it.

"You have an old rag I can use?"

"In the, uh, trailer."

"I'll wait."

She didn't take long.

Aaron rolled up his sleeves and, using the rag to remove the radiator cap, inspected the water level. No surprise, the radiator was bone dry.

"You might have a leak," he told her. "You should get this serviced right away. There's an auto shop in town. Conroy's. Ask your friends, they'll tell you where he is."

"Okay."

Would she do it? She wouldn't get far otherwise.

After filling her radiator with water from the five-gallon jug he carried in the back of his SUV for just this reason, he had her try to start the truck. Luck was on her side, and it turned right over, chugging like an old man having a coughing fit. She definitely needed to see Conroy.

Leaning her head out the window, she removed her ball cap. "Thanks for your help."

Aaron slammed the hood closed and, wiping his hands on the rag, started for his vehicle. "You be careful, you hear?" He stopped and flashed her a smile.

She didn't return it.

Reaching his SUV, he sat behind the wheel and waited for her to pull ahead. Once she had, he radioed in, giving an update and advising the other deputies to keep a lookout for her. That accomplished, he executed a second U-turn and made for the Sanford place.

Even though the girl's name and license plate had checked out, he couldn't stop thinking about her. She was exactly what Aaron had warned Mel to watch for: a stranger in an unfamiliar vehicle. The idea that a slip of a girl was involved with horse rustlers seemed preposterous. Appearances, however, were deceiving and something thieves might use to their advantage.

Turning onto the Sanford's private road, he recalled the young woman removing her ball cap and nearly slammed on the brakes. That was it! The reason she'd looked familiar to him. Her physical description was almost an exact duplicate of Mel's. Blond hair. Brown eyes. Five foot two in her boots. They even had a similar small cleft in their chins.

What were the odds of that?

Chapter Two

"Over here. Another three feet. Wait. No. Up against the wall." Frankie Hartman barked orders in her customary bossy voice.

Mel exchanged looks with her younger sister, Ronnie. As if on cue, they both rolled their eyes and shuffled the table to the exact spot their older sister wanted. Which, it turned out, wasn't so exact.

"Centered beneath the window." Frankie motioned with her hands to demonstrate.

After two more shuffles with the table, Mel and Ronnie were released from their task and instructed to undertake another. There was still a lot to do before the party started at six, including all the decorating.

Mel had brought streamers, a banner, party favors, confetti and a case of champagne. Ronnie's job had been to create a photo collage depicting their father's life from birth to now. Frankie brought the barbecued beef, a family favorite and her specialty dish.

The owner of the Cowboy Up Café, and Frankie's employer, had been kind enough to let them use the covered outdoor patio free of charge. With its built-in misting system, the patio was reasonably comfortable even in ninety-plus-degree temperatures.

The sisters were grateful. With several dozen people expected to attend, they'd definitely needed a large venue, equipped to feed so many mouths. And as if the location wasn't perfect enough, the owner was giving them a discount on the side dishes and beverages.

"Napkins!" Frankie ripped open packages as if the success of the party depended on guests being able to wipe barbecue sauce off their faces and hands.

Mel and Ronnie took their sister's theatrics in stride. Besides being the oldest of the Hartman sisters and a single mother, she was the Cowboy Up Café's head waitress and self-appointed organizer of their dad's party. She'd also stepped in—to the best of her twelve-year-old ability—when the sisters' mother had died over twenty years ago in a horse riding accident. "We're here," a high-pitched voice trilled. "Sorry we're late."

Mel's stepmom was accompanied by two very excited little girls: Frankie's twin daughters.

"We got balloons," Paige announced.

"And string," Sienna added, holding up her booty.

They were dressed alike in matching shorts and tees but were as different as night and day in personalities and features. Tiny, fair-haired Paige took after the Hartmans while tall, doe-eyed Sienna resembled her father, who wasn't and had never been in the picture.

"You wait until Mommy can help," Frankie called from the chair on which she stood, hanging the Happy Birthday banner with Ronnie's assistance.

Mel went over to the girls and scooped them both into her arms. They squirmed and giggled and squealed, loving the attention while pretending not to.

"Let us go," they protested.

"Kisses first."

The girls gleefully obliged.

"Can I help?" Mel asked. Blowing up balloons and taping them to the backs of chairs sounded more fun than laboriously writing out name tags.

"No scissors," Dolores admonished.

Mel relieved her stepmom of the plastic sack and small helium tank she'd carried in. "Does that apply to me, too?"

"Depends. They're sharp." Dolores wagged a finger at her. "Can I trust you?"

"We'll be careful." Mel winked at the girls

and then led them to one of the tables where they set up a balloon inflation station.

"Me first," Paige insisted.

Mel distributed a package of colorful balloons to each girl while keeping the scissors for herself. "Remember to share and take turns."

Ha! Like that was going to happen.

Of course, the pair was more trouble than help, but that didn't matter. They were having a blast. Mel, too.

As luck would have it, Dolores excelled at writing name tags, and between the four of them, the room quickly took shape. Then again, they were old pros, having done this before. Most recently, they'd organized a wedding reception—for Ray Hartman and his new bride.

Ronnie came to stand beside Mel, having finished with bringing in extra chairs from the storeroom. "This is going to sound terrible."

"What?" Mel asked.

"Is it wrong to miss Mom today?"

"No. Of course not. It's Dad's birthday. A milestone birthday."

"I mean, Dolores is wonderful. I adore her."

"Me, too." Mel didn't think there was a more perfect stepmom around.

Ronnie linked arms with her. "Sometimes, I have trouble remembering Mom. I hate that."

"We were young. Don't feel bad. It happens." Mel surveyed the room. "I think she'd approve of this party. I also think she'd like Dolores."

"She'd be proud of us," Ronnie said with conviction. "And of how Dad always supported us. You know the date of their anniversary was one of the numbers Dad used for his lottery tickets."

Mel laughed. "And to think we gave him such grief for buying tickets every week like clockwork."

"None of us ever thought he'd win."

But, then, he had. Last winter. The amount of the jackpot wasn't staggering, about two hundred thousand dollars after taxes. But for the Hartmans, it was a fortune.

Livestock foremen didn't typically earn a lot. Mel's father gave all he had to his daughters, providing a comfortable, if modest, home and the basic necessities. After he won, he'd divided the money equally between the four of them, using his share to pay for his wedding to Dolores and their honeymoon.

"I almost refused the money," Mel said.

Ronnie drew back. "Me, too."

"He didn't tell me that."

"Because he wanted us to take the money. And, frankly, we needed it. You couldn't have bought Doc Palmer's practice otherwise."

"Probably not."

Shortly after the elderly veterinarian announced his retirement, he'd approached Mel about buying his practice. She'd had to tell him no at first. Calling him the following month had been a dream come true.

"And forget Frankie buying that new house," Ronnie said. "It wouldn't have happened."

"True."

Frankie had been desperate to move out of their dad's place. What new bride wanted to share her home with a stepdaughter and two rambunctious stepgranddaughters? Frankie had

used the money from their dad for a down pay-
ment on a cute house in town and some new
furniture.

"Mom would be really happy for us."

Ronnie sighed contentedly. "She did always
call us her fairy princesses."

If not for a lack of handsome suitors, Mel
thought, she and her sisters were living fairy-
tale existences.

Did Aaron count? Not at the moment. She
didn't let herself imagine "someday" and what
the future might hold for them if circumstances changed. Her energies were best focused on making the monthly payments to Doc
Palmer and all those pesky necessities like food,
clothes, repaying college loans and rent on the
house she shared with Ronnie.

The simple and straightforward arrangement
she had with Aaron was enough for both of
them. At least, that was what Mel repeatedly
told herself. Every time she caught herself falling a little harder for him, she remembered that
he wasn't ready or able to fall for her.

Her nieces came bounding back from showing off to their mother, balloons bobbing in the air behind them as if filled with jumping beans and not helium. Ronnie warned them to be careful, her tone a decent imitation of Frankie's. Dolores chatted amiably while putting the finishing touches on the centerpieces.

Soon, they'd leave for their respective homes to change and freshen up before the party. In Frankie's case, she'd pack the barbecued beef for transport and arrive early to start warming it.

Mel stepped forward, intending to gather the balloon supplies, when all at once her stomach lurched and the floor seemed to ripple beneath her feet.

Convinced she was about to embarrass herself, she muttered, "Be right back," to Ronnie and speed-walked across the patio to the café's main building.

By sheer force of will, she made it to the empty restroom and one of the stalls before losing her lunch. Waiting a few moments to be on the safe side, she slowly rose, the sensation of weakness persisting.

She felt her forehead. No fever. Or sore throat or runny nose. Other than intermittent nausea, she exhibited no other symptoms of the flu bug.

What was wrong with her?

Was it possible…? Could she be…?

No. She and Aaron had always been careful about using protection. Mel could not be pregnant.

Nonetheless, she counted backward. How many days since her last period? The answer sent a spear of alarm slicing through her. How had she not realized she was late? She wasn't *that* busy.

Oh, God! Mel sucked in air, unable to catch her breath. Her skin burned as if she did indeed have a fever.

What would she do if she was pregnant? How would Aaron react? Would he be angry? Disappointed? Blame her? Accuse her of trapping him?

She stumbled out of the stall toward the row

of sinks along the wall. Turning on a spigot, she splashed her face with cool water. It didn't alleviate the panic building inside her. Staring at her worried reflection in the mirror only worsened things.

Drying her face with paper towels from the dispenser, she told herself not to cry. There could be any number of reasons she was late and nauseous. Working ridiculous hours, skipping meals and not getting enough sleep, to name a few. Plus, Mel had a history of being irregular. No sense freaking out until she knew for sure.

With a whoosh, the restroom door flew open and Dolores breezed in. Seeing Mel, she stopped midstep.

"Are you okay?"

"I think I have a touch of the flu."

"Oh, no. I'd hate for you to miss the party, but maybe you should stay home and get some rest. You look awful."

Mel tried to wave off her stepmom's concern, only to rush to the stall she'd vacated minutes earlier. When she finally emerged, shaky but in one piece, it was to find Dolores waiting, arms crossed and brows raised.

"How far along are you?"

Mel's knees, already wobbly, threatened to give out. "What?"

"I have three children of my own. I'm very familiar with morning sickness, even when it comes in the afternoon or evening."

Mel started to object. Dolores's kind expression changed her mind. The older woman wasn't her mother. But she was Mel's friend and, she hoped, a confidant.

"Please don't say anything to anyone. Especially Dad. Until I know for sure."

"Then it's possible?"

"We've been careful."

"I was, too. Both the second and third times." Dolores reached for Mel and gave her a quick but warm hug. "Does the father know?"

Again, Mel thought of Aaron. How would he take the news? When would be the best time to tell him? "No. Not yet."

"Do you love him?"

Mel had expected Dolores to ask the name of the father. This question left her nearly as shaken as the bout of nausea had.

Unable to answer, Mel mumbled an excuse and hurried past Dolores. It was one thing to contemplate her changing feelings for Aaron. Another thing altogether to voice them aloud.

MEL GAVE HERSELF a figurative pat on the back for surviving the past few hours. Shortly after escaping the restroom and Dolores, she'd returned to the patio and been immediately recruited to hang paper lanterns. Thank you, Frankie. After that, they'd all gone home to change clothes and then returned before the party started.

Mel didn't typically procrastinate. It wasn't her style. But her father's birthday just wasn't the time for dealing with potentially huge problems. Like, for instance, a missed period. Not even with someone as compassionate as Dolores.

Seeing the party went off without a hitch,

celebrating with her family, those were her priorities. Tomorrow, she'd purchase the home pregnancy test—in Scottsdale where no one knew her—and hopefully eliminate one potential reason for her nausea.

Now *that* was Mel's style. Every move was calculated in advance and every contingency explored. She liked it that way. Order and purpose equaled confidence and a sense of security.

If she turned out to be pregnant, a highly unlikely probability, she'd talk to Aaron and together they'd devise a new plan using the same equation. A plan that didn't throw both their lives into complete and utter chaos.

"Here's my girl!"

The next instant, Mel was swept up in a fierce embrace.

"Dad!" She giggled and squirmed, not unlike her nieces.

"Thank you for the party," he said, releasing her.

"I can't take the credit. It was Frankie's idea, and she did most of the heavy lifting. But you can thank me for not allowing any Over the Hill and Grim Reaper party favors."

"She couldn't have pulled it off without your help."

"I'm glad you're pleased."

His gaze traveled the room. "Who knew I had this many friends?"

His daughters, for one. Mel's dad had lived and worked in the valley for over thirty-five years. He was liked, if not loved, by many.

Not all the guests had arrived. Most noticeably absent was Theo McGraw, Ray Hartman's boss and owner of The Small Change Ranch. Mel hoped the older gentleman would make it. He suffered from Parkinson's disease, and some days were harder than others.

Also absent, and of more concern to Mel, was Aaron and his family. Perhaps he'd gotten called away on a last-minute emergency. Or, something had happened to his daughter. Mel tried not to obsess, which also wasn't her style. But lately, he was constantly on her mind.

"You're being modest." She patted her father's

generous beer belly. That, and his gray beard, had made him the perfect choice to play Santa Claus at his granddaughters' preschool. "You have lots of friends."

"I'm a fortunate man."

She noticed him watching Dolores. He often did, and the look in his eyes softened as if the mere sight of her melted his heart.

Someday, maybe someone would look at Mel like that. Welcome her home after a hard day at work. Slip into bed with her and wind his arms around her. Someone who didn't cling to the memory of his late wife.

Oh, God! Had she really just thought that? Mel was ashamed of herself. She wasn't normally shallow and unkind. Naturally, Aaron grieved his late wife. It had taken her father years to get over her mother's death.

A group of nearby guests burst out in raucous greeting, distracting her. The source of the commotion became quickly apparent. Aaron, his mother-in-law, Nancy, and daughter, Kaylee, had finally arrived.

A grinning Aaron held Kaylee in his arms, balancing her against his broad chest. The shy little girl buried her face in his shirt when one too many people tugged on her silky curls or pinched her chin. Aaron patted her back with his strong hand and, bit by bit, Kaylee's face emerged.

Aaron could do that. Make a person feel safe and sheltered. Mel had experienced it firsthand.

"Hey, there, birthday boy." One of her father's buddies hailed him. "Get over here before all the barbecued beef is gone."

"See you later, honey."

"Enjoy yourself," Mel said to his retreating back, her attention remaining riveted on Aaron.

Eventually, their eyes locked. That was the usual outcome when someone stared long enough. She should step away. Engage the Powells or other clients of hers in conversation. Help Frankie with the food or Dolores with hosting duties.

She and Aaron had agreed not to draw attention to themselves in public, and here she was doing exactly that. Except, she didn't break eye contact and neither did he. The connection Mel had been feeling lately intensified more and more until it practically sizzled.

Was it the same for him? If so, he gave no indication.

Mel's nieces skipped over to Aaron and Kaylee, high on sugar from fruit punch and blobs of icing swiped from the birthday cake.

"Kaylee, play with us," Paige pleaded with her friend. "We have balloons and bubbles and prizes."

The little girl's features lit up like a ray of sunshine after a storm, and she insisted her father put her down.

Aaron relented, holding her hand as if not quite ready to part with her. Mel was close enough to hear him say, "Don't go far, okay?"

"Okay, Daddy," she parroted in her sweet angel voice.

Mel's nieces immediately grabbed her, and the preschool buddies scampered off, disappearing from sight.

"Are you sure she'll be all right?" Nancy asked Aaron, ready to follow the girls.

Aaron waylaid her by saying gently, "She'll be fine. Frankie Hartman is right there."

The creases permanently etched into Nancy's forehead deepened. "I'm going to get some punch."

By sheer coincidence, or not, the punch bowl was located within a few feet of the game area where the girls were playing. If Aaron realized that, and he probably did, he chose not to address it.

Mel admired him for picking his battles. Nancy could be formidable. A self-defense mechanism, no doubt, from losing her only child at a young age.

Funny that Nancy and Dolores had become close. Then again, Dolores was the nurturing kind, taking the lost and lonely into her care. Hadn't she done that with Mel's father and, a few hours ago in the restroom, with Mel?

What if she was pregnant? Mel had tried hard to keep the thought at bay, but it crept back every few minutes, shouting, "You can't ignore me," in her ear.

As if sensing her distress—was he that tuned in to her?—Aaron glanced her way again. Confused and emotionally overwhelmed, Mel turned and snuck away in search of a quiet place.

Five minutes. That was all she needed. Time enough to collect herself and calm her frayed nerves.

Heading outside the café, she skirted the corner to an old hitching post that was still used today for customers arriving by single horse rather than two hundred of them beneath the hood.

Leaning her forearms on the thick railing, she let the warm breeze blow over her. A thin crescent moon hung in the sky above the mountains, waiting for dusk to fall and the stars to come out. Faint strains of piped-in music drifted to her from the patio.

"Hiding?"

Hearing Aaron's voice, Mel jumped.

"Are you okay?" He strolled over to her, his eyes roaming her face. "What's wrong?"

Did he have to look as good in jeans and a cowboy shirt as he did in his uniform? "Just tired. It's been a long week."

"You need to take better care of yourself." He raised his hand and rubbed a knuckle along her jawline. The tender gesture nearly undid her.

It wasn't like him to break the rules. Her, either. No intimacies away from the motel where they typically met. Boundaries were to be respected.

But, then, she remembered she was two weeks late.

"Aaron." She suddenly wanted to confess everything. The fact she was late. Her increasing feelings for him. Her constant confusion.

Wasn't that what couples did? Communicate?

Except, they weren't a couple. They were sex buddies. At her suggestion and insistence.

"What?" he prodded.

"Nothing." She pushed off the hitching post. "We should get back to the party."

At that moment, an older pickup truck going too fast pulled into the parking lot, its tires squealing. Aaron tracked its slightly slower progress to the back row and the only available spaces.

"Someone you know?" Mel asked.

"If it's who I think it is, I ran into her yesterday." He was no longer Aaron but Deputy Travers. "Do you recognize the truck?"

She shook her head. "I don't think so."

Just then, she heard the truck door slam and watched a young, slim woman navigate the parked vehicles, purpose in her stride. Rather than enter the café through the main entrance, she went directly to the outdoor patio.

"Maybe she's someone's plus one," Mel mused.

"I'll be back," Aaron said, barely acknowledging her.

She'd seen this determination before when he was on the job. Did this stranger have something to do with the horse thefts?

"Wait!" She trotted after him, refusing to be excluded.

She reached the patio moments after Aaron. The young woman stood near the food tables, searching the room. Cupping her hands to her mouth, she shouted, "Where's Ray Hartman? I need to talk to him."

For a wild second, Mel thought the young woman was delivering a singing telegram. Except, she didn't wear a costume. Unless one counted that ratty old ball cap.

"I'm Ray." Mel's father, beaming as if he, too, was expecting a birthday surprise, emerged from the crowd, a heaping plate of food in his hands.

"Do you recognize me?"

"'Fraid not."

"I'm Samantha Egherman." She glared at him. "Your daughter. I'm here for my share of the lottery money."

Bursts of laughter vied with gasps of disbelief.

"Who's that?" someone asked.

"She said she's Ray's daughter," another answered.

"Is this someone's idea of a joke?"

Mel was convinced she'd misheard the young woman. Then, like everyone else in the room, she looked at her father. His expression wasn't one of surprise but rather guilt and resignation.

This couldn't be happening. Samantha Egherman? Mel had never heard the name before.

Her ears started ringing, the sound increasing in volume until it blocked out everything else.

His daughter? That made no sense.

Slowly, Mel's father set his plate on the nearest table. Facing the young woman, he said, "Samantha," as if testing her name.

In that instant, Mel knew the outrageous claim was true. She had a half sister. More than that, her father had apparently known and hadn't told anyone.

Chapter Three

Aaron and the other partygoers watched the train wreck unfolding before them with a mixture of surprise, embarrassment and sympathy for those involved. And, of course, morbid fascination. Ray repeating the young woman's name was the equivalent of two locomotives colliding. Mel's startled cry of distress was the first piece of wreckage flying.

Worried by the unsteady way in which she swayed, Aaron pushed past several people to reach her.

"I got you," he said, grasping her elbow.

"I don't believe it." She lifted her face to his. "I don't want to believe it."

Well, who would? Discovering you had an eighteen-year-old sibling wasn't typically on anyone's bucket list.

"Are you okay? You're shaking."

"Okay? You've got to be kidding." She gave a brittle laugh and then bit back a sob.

"I'm happy to see you, Samantha," Ray said. "Finally. I've been waiting a long time."

The young woman glared at him. "Look. All I want is my money. Then I'll get out of here."

Her money? Aaron thought she had some nerve. Make that a *lot* of nerve. Ray had bought the winning ticket. The money was his to gift to whomever he chose.

"Is she scamming Dad?" Mel obviously didn't see the resemblance between her and Samantha that Aaron had noticed yesterday.

"Just wait." He increased his hold on her. "Give them a minute."

Mel briefly resisted before relenting, which

probably had more to do with Frankie's warning glance than Aaron's advice.

"Why don't you have some supper?" Ray offered Samantha a smile. "You must be hungry. Then we'll go home. Continue this discussion in private."

"I don't want any food," she said, her voice tight.

"All right then." He turned and addressed the entire room. "Thank you everyone for coming and making this birthday special. Please stay and enjoy all this great food. My…daughter—" he glanced at Samantha "—and I are leaving."

After that, Aaron couldn't stop Mel from rushing to join them. Her sisters, Frankie and Ronnie, beat her there.

"Dad," Mel said, "you don't have to do this. You have no proof she's who she says she is."

"I'm sorry."

Aaron wasn't sure which of his daughters Ray was apologizing to and what for.

"Is it true?" Frankie demanded. "Is she our sister?"

Ray's smile faltered. "We'll talk about this at home."

"Yes, it's true," Samantha insisted.

"Oh, God." Frankie blinked rapidly as if that could halt the tears filling her eyes.

"I know you." Ronnie nudged Mel aside and pointed at Samantha. "I've seen you compete. You're a barrel racer. A national junior rodeo champion. You turned professional this year."

Being recognized visibly upset Samantha. She didn't let it faze her, however, and rallied by raising her chin. "I know you, too."

From the rodeo circuit or as her long-lost sister?

Ronnie must have wondered the same thing, for she asked, "Why didn't you say something to me when we met before?"

Samantha's answer was to raise her chin another notch.

People continued to gawk and whisper behind the shields of their hands. A few respectfully inched away. The gaps they left were instantly filled.

Aaron debated whether to don his deputy hat and clear the room or allow things to play out. He wasn't on duty, no crime had been committed and no one was in immediate danger. Unless Mel's fragile state counted.

He took a step forward. The hell with this being the Hartmans' crisis to handle. Mel needed a friend, and he was that first and foremost.

His next step was blocked by Nancy, who held Kaylee's hand in a death grip. "Let's go home, Aaron."

"Not yet." He wasn't leaving without talking to Mel.

"Kaylee's upset."

He glanced down at his daughter, who stared over her shoulder at Mel's nieces, a forlorn expression on her face. If she was upset, it was at having to abandon her friends.

It was on the tip of his tongue to chide Nancy for overdramatizing things. Instead, he nodded at their neighbors who were gathering their things.

"There's Geo and Leslie," he said. "Why don't you ask them for a ride home?"

Nancy frowned, not liking the idea. "What about you?"

"I'll be home soon." Aaron bent and gathered Kaylee close. "I love you, jelly bean."

"I wanna stay, Daddy."

"You'll see your friends at preschool on Monday."

Kaylee pouted. In another minute, she'd be whining. In two minutes, she'd be crying.

"I'll be home in time to tuck you in." Aaron straightened. He'd been ready to promise, then stopped himself. With the demands of his job, he couldn't always be where he wanted, when he wanted, and he hated disappointing Kaylee.

Except, this was personal and not work related. He didn't have to stay.

"Will you tell me a story about Mommy?" she pleaded.

Guilt pricked at him. "Of course."

Nancy wasn't the sole keeper of Robin's memories. Aaron's stories tended to be less eloquently spun than Nancy's, but they were told from the heart. He made sure Kaylee knew how much she'd been adored by Robin and how much Robin had been adored by him.

"Bye, Daddy."

Aaron watched his daughter and Nancy until the patio door closed behind them. By then, thankfully, more guests had left, their tongues wagging, Aaron was sure. A few kindly individuals began clearing tables and packing food. No one had heeded Ray's invitation to stay.

Mel, her sisters and Ray stood shoulder to shoulder, presenting a united front. Samantha, for her part, didn't flinch. She either had a lot of nerve or was desperate.

Because he couldn't just stand around doing nothing, he grabbed a heavy-duty plastic bag and began collecting trash. When Mel noticed him, he mouthed, *You okay?*

She shrugged limply. Her red-rimmed eyes indicated she'd been crying or trying hard not to.

He wished he could comfort her. Wrap his

arms around her. Without conscious effort, he pictured them lying nestled softly together in the aftermath of making love. In those moments, he let himself imagine a life beyond stolen evenings here and there. Unfortunately, the fantasy always vanished the instant he set foot inside his house.

It did now, too, as Samantha continued causing a scene.

"Fine," she spat out. "I'll follow you in my truck." She made for the door, her boots clomping on the concrete floor.

A chagrined Ray hurried after her. He was either escaping the wrath of his wife and daughters or attempting to head off disaster. Perhaps a little of both.

"Are we just going to let them leave?" Mel demanded of her sisters.

"Hell, no," Ronnie and Frankie chorused.

"Maybe you should give them some time alone," Dolores said.

The three sisters blinked at her in disbelief.

She crossed her arms. "I'm serious. And you

know I don't usually put my foot down. Ten minutes, then you can go. For now, let's finish cleaning up."

"What about the girls?" Frankie asked, more to herself than anyone else. "I can't just leave them, and I don't want to take them. For obvious reasons."

All eyes fell to Dolores, who gave an expansive huff.

"Thank you," Frankie said, taking the huff as agreement to help.

"We're not excluding you." Mel at least sounded apologetic for all of them taking terrible advantage of Dolores.

"Meet you at the house," Dolores said. "And tell your father to leave me the car. He can catch a ride with one of you three."

Frankie called after her. "Bring the leftover barbecued beef home. Everything else can be stored in the restaurant cooler."

Dolores stopped midstep. "Anything else?"

"Um...no."

Aaron gave Dolores a lot of credit. She was

coping very well with a difficult and awkward turn of events no one had seen coming. She also wasn't protesting when Mel and her sisters took advantage of her generosity. He hoped they let Dolores know how much they appreciated her.

One by one, people were leaving. He supposed he should hit the road as well—except his legs disobeyed his brain and took him in the direction of Mel. She'd already had a rough time tonight and appeared to have a rougher time in store.

When he neared, she actually brightened as if glad to see him.

"Call me if you need anything," he said in a low voice. "I don't care how late it is."

"Thanks for staying. You didn't have to."

"I wanted to." Glancing around first to make sure they weren't being watched—everyone's attention remained elsewhere—he brushed her hand. "I'm here for you, Mel."

When he would have walked away, she quickly touched his arm. "That means a lot to me."

More stolen moments. They were fast becoming not enough.

Outside, the parking lot was considerably less full than earlier. As Aaron crossed it, raised voices drew his attention. In the back row, Samantha stood beside her junkyard truck, its hood raised. Ray was with her, and the two of them argued bitterly.

Aaron hesitated, reminding himself yet again that this was none of his business. If only the law-enforcement officer in him didn't view the situation differently.

Uttering a low groan of frustration, he changed direction. Mel would probably be mad at him for interfering, but Aaron didn't feel he had any other choice. Here was a powder keg on the verge of exploding if ever he saw one.

"IS THERE A PROBLEM?" Aaron asked.

Samantha's laser-beam glance said *butt out.*

Ray, on the other hand, responded with relief. "Aaron. Samantha's radiator is leaking and her truck won't start. I offered to help."

What Ray left out, but Aaron had picked up on, was that Samantha refused any assistance.

Aaron inspected the engine, Samantha peering over his shoulder. "I'm assuming you didn't drop by Conroy's."

"I would if I had the money," she snapped.

Luckily, Aaron had refilled his water jug the previous night. "My vehicle's parked over there. Be right back."

"I'll pay for the repairs." Ray reached in his pocket for his wallet.

"You got forty thousand dollars in there?" Samantha asked. "Because I figure that's my share. Two hundred thousand dollars split five ways."

Aaron wasn't surprised Samantha knew the amount Ray had won. He'd chosen not to remain anonymous, an option given to winners. As a result, an article had appeared in the local paper, and he'd been interviewed by several TV stations, during which he'd stated his plans for the money. Links to both had made the social media rounds.

In five minutes of online searching, Samantha would have found out everything. Which indicated she'd known about Ray and her sisters or someone else did and told her. Her mother, for instance?

That still didn't explain why she felt entitled to a share of the winnings. Perhaps Mel had been close to the truth when she accused Samantha of scamming her father. If not that, then something else. Aaron hadn't trusted Samantha from the moment they'd met.

He also didn't believe her motives were entirely bad or selfish. She struck him more like a scared kid. He knew from both professional and personal experience fear could drive a person to behave in ways they normally wouldn't.

"I'll give you what's left of the money," Ray said to her.

"How much is that?"

"Let's start with the truck repairs."

By the time Aaron returned with the water jug, Mel and her sisters were flying across the parking lot, bags and containers jostling at their sides. Aaron couldn't help thinking here came the disaster Ray had attempted to head off.

"What's going on?" Frankie demanded, out of breath.

Samantha responded as she had before by going stonily silent.

"Nothing." Ray moved toward the young woman as if to shield her.

It didn't go unnoticed, judging by Mel's widening eyes and Ronnie's narrowing ones.

"You should have told us." Tears roughened Frankie's voice. "We had a right to know."

"Not here," Ray said. "We'll talk at home."

That triggered a loud debate among all the Hartmans. Aaron heard the words "betrayal" and "lied to" uttered more than once.

"Excuse me." He squeezed past Mel with the heavy water jug. Ray had already removed the radiator cap. Using his pocket flashlight,

Aaron verified that the radiator was once again bone dry.

Mel appeared beside him. "You're helping her?"

"I'm assisting a stranded motorist by filling her radiator with water. Not taking sides."

"Sorry. This is tough." She swallowed and looked around. "As you can see, we're all a bit rattled."

"Go slow. Try not to make judgments or rush to conclusions. Give your dad and Samantha each a chance to tell their story."

Mel glanced over at the others, several feet away, and lowered her voice. "I'm not sure who to be angrier at."

"What you're feeling is natural. But it's important you keep listening no matter what."

"You sound like you've been through this before."

"I worked on the Phoenix police force for eleven years and responded to my share of domestic dispute calls."

"Is that what we're having? A domestic dispute?"

He bent, unscrewed the cap on the water jug and lifted it up to the truck. "You're a family with a problem."

"That's putting it mildly." She watched him as he filled the radiator.

Finishing, he set the jug down and called to Samantha. "Jump in there and give it a try."

The young woman fled to the truck cab as if she couldn't get away from the Hartmans fast enough and shoved the key into the ignition. The engine sputtered twice, then started.

"She really does need to get that radiator leak fixed," Aaron said to Ray.

"I'll make sure of it."

Aaron wasn't the least bit disappointed this gathering was over. His part in it, anyway. Soon, he'd be home and telling Kaylee another story about her mother.

"You two are on a first-name basis?" Mel asked.

"I met her yesterday when her truck broke down on the side of the road."

"And you didn't tell me?"

"There was nothing to tell at the time."

"You're right, you're right. I'm sorry." She scrubbed her face with her hands and groaned. "What a mess. I didn't mean to take it out on you."

"I've been subjected to far worse."

"On those domestic dispute calls?"

He was glad to see her mouth curve in the beginnings of a smile and leaned closer. "How you feeling? Stomach still bothering you?"

"Frankly, I forgot about it in all the, um, excitement, shall we say."

Only a few inches separated them. Aaron shifted his weight, closing the distance to almost nothing. If they were alone, and oh how he wished they were, he'd gather her into his arms and kiss her over and over until he'd driven every thought of their respective families from their minds.

"What's going on here?"

They sprang apart, separated by Ray's voice and the surprise lacing it. Turning, they found not only Ray but Mel's sisters staring at them.

"Dammit," Aaron said under his breath. This was his fault. He should have been more careful. He and Mel had been getting laxer and laxer lately.

"Dad," she started, then faltered.

They were spared from having to explain whatever it was her family thought they saw when Samantha's truck suddenly quit running. Her attempts to start it again resulted in a horrible grinding sound.

"Shut it off," Aaron hollered, afraid continued effort might result in severe damage.

Samantha scrambled out of the truck. Her mouth was set in an identical stern line Aaron had seen all three Hartman sisters wearing earlier. He was beginning to think looks weren't the only quality they had in common.

By now, evening had given way to night. Above their heads, the parking lot lights flickered and crackled with an electrical hum. A few daring nighttime insects ventured down from the lights. One had the nerve to tangle in Samantha's hair.

She swatted at it furiously. "What now?"

"I'll call Conroy's in the morning," Ray said. "He'll send the tow truck. You can leave your truck here. No one will bother it."

"And in the meantime?"

"Where are you staying?"

Samantha hesitated, wilting a little under the pressure of being scrutinized. "The inn."

Morning Side Inn, like a lot of establishments in the community, was horse friendly. Behind the main building, the owners had constructed a corral and dirt RV lot for guests to use during their stay, which explained what Samantha had done with her horse and trailer.

The inn was also expensive. If she couldn't afford to pay for her truck repairs, she certainly couldn't afford to stay at the inn for long.

"I can drop you off there later tonight," Ray said. "Once we've finished talking." He fished his keys from his pocket. "Let's meet at the house. Samantha, you can ride with me and Dolores." He turned in a circle and frowned, suddenly realizing his wife had been missing all along.

"No way am I riding with you," Samantha stated frimly. "I'll walk to the inn. It's not far from here."

"I think we should talk tonight," Ray insisted. "The sooner the better."

She scrunched her mouth to the side, debating what to do. Suddenly, she pointed at Aaron. "I'll ride with him."

Reactions ranged from surprise to displeasure to resistance. Aaron didn't blame them. He'd already intruded enough on what was a private matter. Besides, someone else needed him more. "I can't take you. My daughter's expecting me home any minute."

"What if I drive you?" Frankie asked Samantha.

The young woman raised her chin like before. "If he doesn't take me, I'm not going."

Aaron had witnessed this same stubbornness

in Mel, usually when she refused to give up on a sick or injured animal. Also, the one time he'd broached the subject of them dating like a regular couple.

She'd insisted what they had suited them both. Why complicate matters? Lately, he'd been thinking he should have argued more. She deserved better than what they had, even if she didn't believe so. And he had started wanting more, even if he refused to admit it.

Their gazes briefly connected, and he wondered if she also ever reconsidered their arrangement.

"This is probably best handled by your family," Aaron said to Samantha.

"They're not my family," she contradicted him. "I already have one. My mom and dad and two brothers."

Again, everyone except Ray seemed taken aback by the news, eyes widening and jaws going slack. What other secrets was he keeping?

Mel was the first to speak. "Maybe you should drive her to Dad's house. We certainly can't keep standing here all night." Before Aaron could refuse, she added, "I'll go with you."

No one brought up the obvious. As deputy sheriff, Aaron was familiar with the town and didn't need directions. Could Mel be trying to find time alone with him? As alone as they could be with another person sitting three feet away.

That wasn't why Aaron ultimately agreed to drive Samantha. It was the scared look on her face. She was a kid in trouble, though no one else apparently saw it. If his daughter ever needed help, he hoped a responsible and trustworthy person like himself stepped in.

An unofficial vote was taken, and Aaron found himself in his SUV with Mel in the front, Samantha in the back and a heavy silence surrounding them. Guess he'd been wrong about Mel's motives.

"Take a left," she instructed when they reached the parking lot exit. "Turn east onto Harvest Street."

Traffic was never heavy in Mustang Valley,

with the exception of holidays when the whole town came out to celebrate. With each occasional vehicle passing them in the opposite direction, the interior of the SUV was illuminated by oncoming headlights.

Aaron caught quick glimpses of Mel's profile. She was just as scared as Samantha. He also understood why—her entire life was changing—and was glad he'd come along for her, too.

Chapter Four

The Hartman home was about four miles past where the paved road leading out of town ended and the dirt road began. Mel's parents had built it soon after her father accepted a head wrangler position at The Small Change Ranch, using the entirety of their meager savings for construction. The house was a short distance from the ranch and until recently, her father had ridden to work every day.

He told people the reason he quit was because his favorite horse had been retired and put to pasture, not that his arthritis had worsened. Mel didn't have the heart to dispute him. Her father was a proud man.

"What about your friends?" Aaron asked Samantha, glancing again in the rearview mirror. Mel noticed he'd been doing that a lot during the drive.

"What about them?" Samantha said tersely.

"Are they expecting you tonight?"

"No."

"Have you called them?"

Samantha gave another terse reply and slouched into her seat.

Mel frowned. Really? Aaron was attempting chitchat? And who were these supposed friends of Samantha's anyway?

"What if they're worried?" Aaron asked.

"You always this nosy?"

"Comes with the job."

Gauging by her tone, Samantha didn't like Aaron better than Mel or the rest of them. So why insist on him driving her?

The two had another brief exchange, and Mel's irritation escalated. Perhaps because

Aaron had obviously learned details about Samantha and Mel knew nothing. None of them did. Except her father. He'd known her name, at least. And that she existed. He was certainly on good terms with Samantha's mother. Or, had been at one time.

A sister. Mel had *another* sister. She silently did the math. Her dad and Samantha's mom must have met one, no, two years after Mel's mother died.

Pain burned inside her chest. Plenty of people would defend her father, saying he hadn't been married when he and Samantha's mom met and that two years was a reasonable period to mourn before entering into a new relationship.

Only it didn't feel reasonable to Mel. The man she remembered had been devastated to his very core, blaming himself for a freak riding accident he couldn't have prevented even if he was there when it happened. Afterward, Mel's father could barely drag himself out of the house to buy groceries or take the girls to a school function. He'd gone to work every day only because he'd needed to support his family—what remained of it.

Date? Engage in dinner conversation? Laugh? Have sex? It was beyond Mel's ability to take in, and she hugged her middle.

"Cold?" Aaron asked, already adjusting the air conditioning.

"I'm fine."

She quietly fumed. Why hadn't her father told them about Samantha? It made no sense. Having a child with another woman was a big deal. Life altering. Did he think they'd never find out or not care if they did?

"Why now?" The words erupted from her, and she twisted in her seat to confront Samantha. "Why pick today of all days to suddenly show up?"

"Does it matter?" Samantha stared out the passenger window.

"You crashed my dad's birthday party and demanded forty thousand dollars. I'd say I'm owed an explanation. All of us are."

Samantha's head snapped around. "You

haven't wanted an explanation for eighteen years. I could ask you, why now?"

"Wait just a minute. I had no idea—"

"And that's my fault?"

Mel opened her mouth to protest, realized the futility of it and instead swung back around, her tenuous hold on her temper threatening to break. She did not like this person. This stranger. This interloper.

"He's not the great guy you think he is," Samantha said.

"How do we even know you're his daughter? You could be making the whole thing up."

"Did he act like I was making it up?"

Mel wanted to scream. This could not be happening. It had to be a mistake. A terrible joke gone horribly wrong.

The next instant, Aaron's hand reached across the console for hers.

"Relax," he said softly. "There's no use getting upset."

She should have shaken him off and would have if not for the warmth flowing through her and the knotted muscles in her neck slowly loosening. Damn him for sensing what she needed, which at the moment was a nonjudgmental friend in her corner.

Opening her fist, she linked her fingers with his, marveling at this tiny intimacy. For the first time away from the motel, they were holding hands, and she had to admit, the sensation was nice. It was also something she could get used to if she let herself.

"You two together?" Samantha asked from behind them.

Mel snatched her hand away, the remark hitting much too close to home for her liking. "It's not like that. We're just friends."

"Right."

Mel imagined Samantha rolling her eyes.

Aaron grinned and shrugged, not the least bit bothered.

If only Mel could be as unconcerned as him. But she couldn't. Not when she secretly, sort of, wanted to take their relationship to the next level. Or was that back a level since most couples began by dating, not sleeping together whenever the time was right and they felt like it.

Her hand drifted to her belly. Could she be pregnant? If yes, their relationship might jump ahead two or three levels overnight.

She remembered her plan to purchase a home pregnancy test tomorrow. Well, so much for that. With Samantha's appearance and her outrageous demand, the day, and entire weekend, had taken a crazy turn. She'd be lucky to get to the store by Tuesday.

One good thing, she hadn't felt nauseous for a while now. Perhaps it was the flu after all.

Without being told, Aaron turned the SUV onto the road leading to her father's house.

"I've been here before," he said in response to Mel's raised brows. "Your house, too."

"Make the rounds a lot?"

"I like to keep tabs on certain people."

Did he? "Is that also part of the job?"

His response was a smile.

What did that mean? That he personally watched out for her and her family? Why, for heaven's sake? Sure, he cared for her, but not like that.

"How much farther?" Samantha demanded with growing impatience.

"Not long."

Beyond the next rise, the front porch light on the Hartman house came into view. Aaron increased his speed slightly, and the SUV bumped over several potholes carved into the road.

Mel's stomach abruptly lurched. Well, so much for thinking she'd recovered. Leaning back, she closed her eyes and hoped she didn't throw up in the SUV.

"You all right?" Aaron let up on the gas, slowing the vehicle.

"Just nerves."

"It wasn't nerves yesterday."

She sent him a sideways glance, silently warning him to drop the subject. Thankfully, he did.

A few minutes later, they pulled into the driveway, and Aaron parked to the side in order to let Mel's father pass them. He and her sisters had been following close behind the entire drive.

Mel thrust open her door, more than ready to get out. She was less enthusiastic about what lay ahead.

"Thanks again." She attempted a feeble smile. "For everything." There'd be no more hand holding for her and Aaron. Not tonight and not with Samantha watching.

"Call me later," he said, repeating his earlier request.

"I will." A phone call that had nothing to do with arranging an evening at the motel. Their first of that sort, Mel mused.

Realizing Samantha hadn't moved, she said, "We're here," then waited, feeling like she'd stated the obvious.

Samantha chewed on her lower lip, not moving. Mel wanted to ask what was wrong. After making a huge scene at the café, she couldn't believe Samantha had suddenly developed cold feet.

"I'm not going inside." Samantha hitched her chin at Aaron. "Not without him."

"No!" Mel managed to get out, a second ahead of Aaron.

"Samantha," he said, "it's getting late. I have to go home to my daughter."

By now, Mel's sisters had disappeared into the house. Her father waited beside the open garage door.

Samantha spoke so quietly, Mel wasn't sure she'd heard correctly.

"Please. You're the only person I know here." After a beat, she added, "You helped me before."

Aaron considered briefly, ultimately relenting and unbuckling his seat belt. "Only for a few minutes."

"That's not a good idea." Mel was thinking of her family's reaction.

"She's young and all alone."

Apparently, Mel's corner wasn't the only one Aaron was in. He'd taken a position in Samantha's, too. Mel was torn between being furious at him and touched by his concern.

Samantha's shoulders slumped with relief. So,

she did have cold feet after all. Hard to believe after the brazen way she'd confronted them at the party.

Aaron got out of the SUV, followed by Samantha. He waited for Mel to join them before heading into the garage. She made a point of walking on his other side and slightly in front. This was her family. Their house. She would lead.

"You need something, Deputy?" her father asked when they neared.

Samantha cut in before Aaron could respond. "He stays or I leave."

Aaron lifted a shoulder in apology. "I promise to keep my mouth shut and any opinions to myself."

Mel's father didn't look happy. She found it hard to sympathize despite defending him earlier. He was in large part responsible for this mess.

Samantha hung close to Aaron as the four of them paraded single file through the laundry room, along the short connecting hall and into the kitchen where Frankie and Ronnie waited. They, too, showed surprise and displeasure at seeing Aaron.

"What's he doing here?" Frankie glowered accusingly.

Mel's father dropped his phone, wallet and keys on the counter. "Samantha invited him."

"Do we need a mediator?"

Rather than reply, he addressed the group. "Anyone want a cold drink before we get started?"

Mel thought she might want a stiff drink but decided that wasn't a good idea.

"I'll get them." She recruited Ronnie to help. When her sister wasn't looking, she grabbed a couple of the peppermint candies her father kept in the drawer for his frequent indigestion.

The moment Aaron was finished with his phone call to his mother-in-law, letting her know he'd be late, people began sitting at the dining-room table. The area was separated from the kitchen by a long breakfast bar and a trio of oak bar stools. Frankie switched on the overhead light. The normally cozy glow did nothing to improve their collective serious mood.

Aaron waited for Samantha to pick a seat at the end of the table before pulling out the chair beside her. Since he'd been invited by Samantha, it was natural he'd sit beside her. That was what Mel told herself, anyway.

By the time Mel finished distributing glasses of ice water, Ronnie had already claimed a seat. That left one empty chair, which just happened to be on Aaron's other side.

All attention was focused on her when she sat. Her *and* Aaron. Eventually, she'd have to answer their unspoken questions. Like what was going on between them and for how long?

Not tonight, however. For in the next instant, everyone's gaze turned to Samantha.

AARON COULDN'T REMEMBER when he'd last felt this out of place. Maybe in the attorney's office when Robin, her head partially shaved from a recent medical procedure, had insisted they update their living trust and her medical directive.

Or when he'd told Nancy he was taking a job in Mustang Valley.

It wasn't just the invisible daggers being fired at him from all directions or the furious expressions on every Hartman face. Nor was it being dragged into the middle of a family dispute. Aaron had dealt with plenty of those during his law-enforcement career.

What made him uncomfortable was the fact that, in this particular dispute, he was a participant. An unwilling one, and only by association with Samantha, but a participant nonetheless.

Maybe he should leave after all. Forget Samantha needing an ally. But Mel looking ready to fall apart at the seams kept him rooted to his chair.

Guessing from her stiff posture and refusal to acknowledge him, she didn't appreciate his assistance. Hopefully later, when she'd calmed down, she would see he'd been trying to help.

Please don't take long, he thought, certain it would. Messes like this one, almost twenty years in the making, required more than a single evening of discussion to resolve.

For one brief second, he considered locating Mel's fingers beneath the table and folding them inside his. He came to his senses at the precise moment Frankie's searing gaze elevated to nuclear.

Great. What effect was this going to have on their daughters' friendship? None, he hoped.

Aaron suffered another pang of guilt—he'd lost track of how many tonight. Poor Kaylee. That she always forgave him when he came home late and missed story time was a minor miracle and one he didn't take for granted.

Ray finally broke the silence, chuckling nervously. "Where to start?"

His glance traveled to each of his daughters, one after the other, lighting last on Samantha. If he was hoping to promote a camaraderie among them, they were having none of it.

"I met Samantha's mother...I guess it was a couple years after your mom died. I accidentally stepped on her foot while picking out tomato plants in the garden department at the Home Warehouse Store. She asked for my advice on which was the best variety to grow in patio pots."

"Carrie Anne," Samantha said, her voice bowstring tight. "Her name is Carrie Anne."

"Yes. Of course. Carrie Anne."

It seemed Ray had the ability to slight all of his daughters without trying hard.

Drawing in a deep breath, he continued wreaking more emotional havoc with his story.

"We got to talking and before we knew it, an announcement came on the speakers that the store was closing. I asked her, Carrie Anne, to go for coffee with me, convinced she'd turn me down. I was, am, older than her, and she was so pretty. Plus, I was out of practice. When she said yes, I nearly lost my nerve. But she laughed at my jokes and smiled at me like she was interested in what I had to say."

All of them, Aaron included, sat spellbound. Did Mel and her sisters wonder what quality Carrie Anne had possessed, other than looks,

that turned their grief-stricken father into a flirt
who asked random women he met in the garden
department out for coffee?

"We didn't date long." Ray avoided making eye contact with anyone. "A few months.
I wasn't ready to commit and neither was she,
for that matter. She'd just broken up with her
boyfriend and was feeling insecure about herself. Eventually, we came to our senses and
parted ways. No hard feelings. She called me
four months later to tell me she was pregnant
and intended to have the baby."

Beside him, Aaron heard Mel suck in air
through clenched teeth. He was thinking Carrie Anne had duped Ray a little by waiting so
long to break the news and denying him any say
in the matter. Was Mel thinking that, as well?

"Carrie Anne was very sensible about the
whole thing," Ray said. "I offered to get married, but she'd hear none of it. She insisted I'd
proposed out of duty and was still grieving my
wife, and that you girls were in no emotional
state to accept a stepmother, much less a new

baby sibling. I went along, for her sake and mine. I didn't want her missing out on the opportunity to meet the right guy.

"Turns out, I was right. Carrie Anne eventually reconciled with her boyfriend. After they got married, he asked to adopt Samantha. They were in love. Planned on having children. I thought it made sense."

Samantha didn't contradict Ray, which gave Aaron reason to believe the story was true.

"Did you love her?" Mel asked in a quiet voice. "Carrie Anne?"

Ray grimaced. "Whatever I say, I'm going to sound like a jerk."

Aaron related. He struggled with the same thing when it came to him and Mel and defining his feelings for her.

Did she notice the similarities between their situation and her father and Carrie Anne's and appreciate the irony? Both he and Ray grieved late wives and were reluctant to commit. Both had children who would be affected by and possibly resent their father's new relationship.

"If Carrie Anne and I had met a few years later," Ray said, "if she hadn't been in love with another man, who can say what might have been? But things were what they were, and I'm convinced they worked out for the best."

"Best for whom?" Samantha asked.

"Your mother seems happy. She always indicated to me that you were, too."

"You've spoken to Carrie Anne?" Mel's voice cracked.

"Periodically. She's kept me updated."

Samantha glowered at him. "You didn't speak to me."

"That was your mother and father's choice. Didn't she tell you?"

"She said you didn't want any contact with me."

"Really?" Ray looked surprised. "She told me you didn't want any contact with me."

Samantha stiffened, obviously not liking this revelation.

Ray addressed Mel and her sisters. "Carrie Anne and her husband decided when Sam was sixteen, she'd be informed about me and given my phone number to call if she wanted. Until then, Sam was raised believing Carrie Anne's husband was her father."

"How could you have agreed to that?" Mel flushed in outrage. "She was your child."

"I had my hands full raising you girls. You were my priority. Sam had a mother."

"Not so full you couldn't find time to date."

"I get that you're mad, honey. But I didn't go out with Carrie Anne to hurt you. I was lonely and sad. Try to understand."

"Why would I contact you?" Samantha apparently wasn't finished throwing punches. "You didn't want me when my mom got pregnant and left her to raise me alone. Just to get out of paying child support."

Aaron doubted Ray was required to pay anything as he'd waived his parental rights.

"Now, that's not true," Ray said, shocking everyone. "I gave your mother money every year up until a few months ago when you turned eighteen. I have the canceled checks to prove it."

"Why would she lie to me?" Samantha shook her head in confusion. "That makes no sense."

"Why not?" Mel said. "She lied to you about your real father."

"Enough." Ray sent Mel a warning look.

To Samantha, he said, "You'll have to ask your mother about that."

She thrust back in her chair, an angry scowl on her face. Aaron suspected more and more that Samantha was on the outs with her parents, particularly her mother.

Ray studied the young woman, his expression changing as if seeing her for the first time, which wasn't far from the truth. "Is that why you refused to talk to me? Because of the child support?"

"You didn't want me," she repeated with considerably less conviction.

"Honestly, Sam. You had a much better life with your parents than you would have had with me. It's not that I don't love you—"

"Do you?"

"I could. I *will* love you once we get to know

each other." Ray paused, seeming to search for what to say. "I did as much right by you as your mother would allow me and, honestly, as much as I was capable of at the time."

Samantha's expression changed, and she suddenly appeared younger than her eighteen years.

"I'd like to get to know you now," Ray said. "If you're willing. Broke my heart two years ago when you refused to call."

"Forgive me if I'm still a little confused." Mel peered around Aaron at Samantha. "Your mother wasn't honest with you. She hid your real father from you and conveniently forgot to mention he paid child support. And instead of connecting with him when you had the chance, getting his side of the story, you blamed him for abandoning you. Now, you show up out of the blue, demanding money that you have no right to. My mind is boggled."

"He gave you each a share. Why not me? I'm his biological daughter."

"But not his legal daughter."

Mel's harsh but true reply visibly rippled among the others at the table.

"What did your mother have to say about you coming here?" Ray asked.

Samantha was slow to respond. "She...doesn't know."

As Aaron had expected.

"And don't call her." Samantha pointed at Ray.

"Because she wouldn't approve?" Mel asked.

Ray jumped quickly to Samantha's defense. "Give the girl a break."

"Dad! She's being unreasonable. And thinking only of herself. This isn't your fault. Not all your fault, anyway. She's out of line."

"I need the money." Samantha ignored Mel, addressing Ray instead. "You owe me."

He blew out a long breath. "The fact is, most of the money's been spent."

Samantha's eyes widened. "Already? I don't believe you."

Two hundred thousand dollars might seem like a huge sum. But in Aaron's experience of dealing with a catastrophic illness and premature birth of a baby, it could be spent in a week. Thank goodness for health insurance.

"I could try to scrape together a few thousand dollars," Ray offered.

"That's not enough." Samantha's pout returned. "I need more. A lot more."

"Why? For what?"

"Big John." Samantha promptly burst into racking sobs.

Frankie sprang up and put a comforting arm around the young woman's shoulders.

Mel, on the other hand, must've reached her limit. Pushing away from the table, she left through the Arcadia door that lead to the patio. Aaron thought there might have been tears in her eyes.

Ronnie returned to the kitchen for another round of ice water while Ray stared off into space.

Aaron debated for several seconds before getting up and following Mel outside. The hell with what anyone thought of them.

He found her sitting in one of the lawn chairs,

her back to him. At his approach, she glanced up, then quickly looked away.

"Mind if I join you?"

She acquiesced with a sigh.

Aaron took that as a yes and dropped into the chair next to hers.

Mel needed no prompting, her words coming out in a rush. "I get it. She's young and a victim of circumstances beyond her control. Her parents, my dad included, made some crummy decisions. She deserves our sympathy and understanding. But that doesn't stop me from being mad. At her. At Dad. At Carrie Anne whatever-her-last-name-is."

"You have good reason. Your dad lied to you."

Mel let her face fall into her hands. "How could he?"

"Be honest. Would you and your sisters have accepted a stepmom and baby sister?"

Her head popped up. "I love Dolores."

"You're an adult. What about when you were ten?"

"Twelve. I'd have been twelve at the time."

"Would you have accepted Carrie Anne and Samantha then?"

"Well, we'll never know, will we? Because I wasn't given the opportunity."

He let her stew in silence for a few minutes.

Eventually, she said, "I don't have any money to give her even if I wanted to. I used it all to purchase my vet practice."

"That problem is your dad's to solve. Not yours."

"Do you think he didn't give her a share because he'd have had to explain it to me and Frankie and Ronnie?"

Aaron shook his head. "If I were to venture a guess, I'd say he already gave far more financially to Samantha than he was obligated to."

"Hmm." Mel let that sink in. "Sorry I was short with you earlier."

"I didn't notice." He smiled.

"I realized you weren't taking her side."

"It's a tough situation. Tempers are bound to flare."

"You've done nothing but try to help."

"I told you before, Mel, you can count on me."

Because her hands were clasped in her lap, Aaron rested a hand on her knee. After a moment, she closed her eyes.

"We should talk."

"I agree," Aaron said.

"In a day or two."

"Let me know when. I'll make myself available."

They had plenty to say to each other. His hand on her knee was evidence of that.

The door suddenly slid open, and Frankie stuck her head out. Mel pulled her knee away, but Aaron didn't think her concern was necessary. Frankie probably hadn't seen anything in the darkness.

"Dolores just got here with the girls," she said. "And I have an idea for what to do about Samantha. So, get in here now, you two." She ducked back inside.

Aaron rose first and assisted Mel to her feet. They didn't immediately separate.

"I'm sorry you got caught up in all this," she said softly.

"Don't worry about it."

The wedge of light shining from the door provided just enough light for him to see the regret in her eyes and something else. Something he couldn't pinpoint.

"What's happening with us?" she whispered.

Frankie hollered at them from inside the house, preventing Aaron from answering. Not that he knew what to say.

Chapter Five

"Her horse is injured," Frankie said, nodding at Samantha. "A torn ligament. That's why she wants the money. Not for herself."

Mel didn't see the logic. Wasn't wanting money for one's horse the same as wanting it for oneself? Frankie didn't usually split hairs, which Mel took to mean her sister sympathized with Samantha.

She studied the table. The family had resumed their former seats, with the exception of Mel's father. Dolores now occupied his chair, and he stood behind her, his hands resting on her shoulders. She periodically glanced up at him with love and support. Her father, as usual, returned her affection.

Mel increased her scrutiny. Strange that Dolores didn't appear upset or shocked to learn her husband had a daughter from a previous affair or even that the daughter suddenly showed up. If anything, she was...

He'd told her! Dammit. Nothing else made sense.

Mel didn't like the anger rising inside her but was unable to stop it. How could her father have confided in his new wife and not in his own daughters? The ones most affected.

Frankie settled more comfortably into her chair, preparing to lead the discussion. Mel tried not to be angry at her, either, just because she "had an idea what to do" and wasn't furious like Mel.

The girls were in the spare room, tucked into bed for the night but probably giggling. They'd stay over, with Frankie returning for them in the morning. Dolores had furnished the spare room with their various grandchildren specifically in mind.

"When did the injury happen?" Mel asked Samantha.

"Six weeks ago."

She encountered these type of injuries on a regular basis. "It's not the end of the world. I'm sure your vet recommended a treatment course."

"Two vets," Samantha clarified. "The first one said I should pasture Big John for six months. The second said I could bring him along sooner but to take it slow."

Both schools of thoughts had their merits. Which one was best depended on the nature of the tear and the horse. In Mel's opinion, the treatment of a torn ligament, even a small tear, shouldn't be rushed or else the horse risked permanent injury.

"Samantha's trying to qualify for the National Finals Rodeo," Ronnie said. "Her horse is…was her best chance. Without him, she'll have to quit competing."

"Can't she use another horse? Borrow one?"

Mel didn't see the problem. "She must have friends who are barrel racers."

"There isn't one available," Ronnie said. "Not from a friend and not of the caliber she'd need to consistently win."

"Ah." That explained the demand for money. "She wants to buy a new horse."

"Not exactly," Ronnie admitted.

Mel's younger sister would identify with Samantha's problem. She'd come close to qualifying for the NFR herself more than once in her barrel-racing career, always falling just short. Retiring from the circuit without a NFR championship to her name was her biggest regret.

A bell went off inside Mel's head, and the last several minutes started to make sense. "You want me to treat her horse."

"You're a good vet," Frankie said.

"And no better than those other two, I'm sure."

"You haven't examined the horse. Maybe you should hold off until you have."

"It's July. She has, what? Four months left to qualify? No horse is going to sufficiently recover from a torn ligament before then. And does it really matter? How close are you to qualifying, anyway?"

Samantha shrugged. "I can do it. If I start competing again in the next few weeks."

"And win," Mel added. "On an unfamiliar horse."

She knew a little about barrel racing from watching Ronnie compete through the years. It was an arduous sport that required skill, talent, drive and a perfect partnership between horse and rider. Also, sufficient resources. Barrel racing wasn't cheap. Ronnie had worked part-time during high school to help their father pay her expenses. After graduation, she'd worked full-time, with half her salary going toward competing.

Surely another reason Samantha wanted the money. To pay her hefty costs.

"It's always sad when an animal is injured," Mel said, "and I feel for you. But, there's no money left from Dad's winnings and not much I can do for you that your own vets haven't."

"Can or will?" Samantha asked, her voice sharpening.

"I'm not a miracle worker, and I won't be held responsible if your horse ends up permanently lame."

She snuck a peek at Aaron beside her. Did he think she was being too hard on Samantha? He'd grown up with horses and these days enjoyed recreational riding, but he wasn't a hardcore enthusiast like everyone in Mel's family.

His expression revealed nothing other than mild curiosity. Mel wanted to think she cared little about his opinion and was taken aback by how much she did. If they were alone, she'd ask him what she should do.

"I think we can help Samantha," Frankie said. "She deserves it after all. She's missed out on a relationship with Dad and us her whole life."

"Did you not hear the same story I did?" Mel asked. "She *chose* not to have a relationship with him, *and us*, these last two years."

"She was hurt."

"And she's not the only one." Mel hated that

she was on the verge of tears. "I'm not trying to be mean. Really. But you can't make us responsible for her mom and our dad's screwup. How is that fair?"

Frankie wore the same struggling-to-be-patient face she frequently did with her daughters. "How is it fair that Samantha suffer when we can help her? Won't you at least examine her horse?"

Mel's father spoke for the first time since they'd resumed the meeting. "You're angry. Who wouldn't be? I should have told you girls about Samantha a long time ago. Whenever the right moment arose, I came up with an excuse. Eventually, I stopped looking for moments."

"That's not a good enough reason, Dad." Mel shook her head. "It's actually a pretty bad one."

"You girls loved your mother so much." Sorrow filled his eyes. "I didn't want you to hate me."

"So, instead, you were grossly unfair to Samantha."

Had Mel just defended Samantha? More likely, she was just angry at her father.

She stared across the table, not recognizing the man standing there. Her father, the one who'd raised her, had been kind and good and loving and honest. He didn't deceive people, regardless of the reason.

Yet, he had. For more than eighteen years. How could Frankie and Ronnie not feel the same bitterness and disappointment she did?

Mel tamped down her emotions and faced Frankie.

"Don't make me out to be a terrible person just because I'm upset. I think we can all agree Dad hiding the fact he had a daughter with another woman is hard to understand and difficult to forgive."

"You don't want me, either," Samantha ground out.

Mel groaned in frustration. Was everyone intentionally taking what came out of her mouth the wrong way? "That's not what I said."

"You implied it."

Had she? Mel rubbed her throbbing forehead. This discussion was gaining momentum and going entirely in the wrong direction.

"You've known about us for a while. My sisters and I only just learned about you less than two hours ago. We deserve a break. Some time to adjust."

"I agree," Frankie said. "Which is another good reason for what I'm going suggest. Not only can we help Samantha, we'll have a chance to get better acquainted with her and her with us."

She made it sound like a meet the teacher night at school.

"Dad, Ronnie, Samantha and I talked while you were outside with Aaron, and we're in agreement."

Mel doubted she was going to like what came next. "I'm all ears."

"Okay." Frankie squared her shoulders. "Here's the plan in a nutshell. Starting tomorrow, Samantha will stay with me. In exchange for room and board, she'll help around the house. Maybe, if things go well, she can watch the girls when I'm at work. Take them to and pick them up from preschool."

"She's going to remain in Mustang Valley?" Mel asked.

"You'll treat her horse. At no cost."

"It's not the money. I already said, there's no way the horse can improve sufficiently to compete in time for Nationals."

"Ronnie will let Samantha use one of her horses in the meantime."

Mel had to swallow her shock. Ronnie had purchased those two horses with the money from their father in the hopes of selling them for a profit. She was sacrificing a lot.

"Lastly, Dad will cover Samantha's competition costs and see to it that she gets to and from the rodeos." Frankie finished with a satisfied smile.

Everyone looked at Mel and waited, as if the entire success of this harebrained scheme depended on her.

"I can't stop any of you from doing what you want."

Frankie's smile faltered. "Are you saying you won't treat the horse?"

"I'd like to sleep on it."

"Come on, Mel. You're being stubborn."

"She's not," Dolores said, contributing for the first time. "It's a reasonable request. You're the ones who are out of line, expecting her to agree on the spot."

Mel sent her stepmom a grateful look.

Dolores began gathering water glasses, signaling the end of the meeting.

"There's still a lot to discuss," Frankie objected.

"I'd like to go home." Mel was tired, the most tired she'd been in weeks. Months. "It's been a long day."

As the last word escaped, she realized she didn't have a vehicle here. She'd driven with Ronnie to the café and with Aaron from there to her father's. Her truck was at home. Son of a—

"I can drop you off." Aaron checked his watch. "I need to leave myself."

She couldn't ride with him. What would her family say? They were already suspicious. Then again, with the way she felt now, the heck with her family and what they thought.

"Fine."

"Samantha?" Aaron asked. "You want to come with us?"

"I'll take her," Mel's father volunteered. This time, Samantha didn't refuse. "Frankie and Ronnie, you can ride with us and pick up your vehicles. The Morning Side Inn is right down the road from the café."

Mel's house was a ten-minute drive at most from her father's. She and Aaron spent the first eight minutes in silence. But Mel couldn't keep quiet after that.

"Do you think I'm being unreasonable?"

"Not at all."

He sounded genuine, which relieved her greatly, then brought her to tears. "I don't know what's wrong with me." She wiped at her damp eyes.

"You've had a rough day, and you're not feeling well."

Oh, yeah, thought Mel. That, too. She'd momentarily forgotten about her pregnancy-like symptoms.

"Don't be so hard on yourself."

Aaron didn't walk her to the door, not that she'd expected him to. But, before she got out of his SUV, he did take her hand and raised it to his lips for a lingering kiss.

"Good night, Mel." He met her eyes across the darkness.

"Um, night." She reclaimed her hand.

In a half-daze, she hurried up the walk to her house, thinking Aaron kissing her hand was the most romantic gesture any guy had ever made.

Oh, yeah. They really did need to talk.

UNLESS THERE WAS an emergency that couldn't possibly wait, Mel took Sundays off. It was her one full day of rest and relaxation and, normally, she relished it, sleeping in until seven or even later.

But today, she'd gotten up early and wandered the empty house, too restless and nervous to stay in one place long. Last night's events were on her mind, though not as prominently as her possible pregnancy. Still no period. Off and on nausea. Overwhelming tiredness. Ready to cry at the drop of a hat. It was getting harder and harder to ignore the signs.

Thankfully, Mel had the place to herself. Ronnie had left at daybreak for Powell Ranch to ready her two barrel-racing horses. Samantha would meet her there after breakfast and, together, they'd choose the right horse for her.

Grabbing a second cup of coffee, which wasn't helping her anxiety—she tried not to think how bad caffeine was for a baby—Mel padded outside to the shaded patio.

She had always loved the backyard. It was her main reason for choosing this house over the other available rentals in town. To her right was a perfect view of the McDowell Mountains and Pinnacle Peak. To her left, and beyond the neighbors' houses, stretched endless desert. The fenced yard, with its see-through rails, allowed her to view both to her heart's content.

She'd always thought that someday, when her schedule allowed it, she'd adopt a rescue dog or two. The yard was designed for romping and playing, and she missed having pets. The yard was also custom-made for children. A family was also in her "someday" plans, along with a caring and devoted husband.

It seemed, however, she might be having children sooner than expected. One, at least. And no caring and devoted husband.

Mel leaned back in the wicker lounge chair and closed her eyes. Later today, regardless of what happened, she'd drive to Scottsdale and buy an early-pregnancy test. Then, she could concentrate on Aaron and their evolving relationship, which seemed bound to change whether she was pregnant or not. Equally pressing was Samantha, and Frankie's plan for the entire Hartman clan to help out their surprise half sister.

Mel decided assessing her priorities was a

good stepping-off place. Naturally, her practice topped the list. It was more than a job or a salary to Mel. It was her dream. Her passion. Her reason for eagerly embracing each day. Her goal was to be as successful as her predecessor, if not more so, and a valuable part of the community.

When she did eventually have a family of her own, she'd need to be able to help support them, if not be the sole provider. Her father had taught Mel independence and the value of hard work. He'd also taught her the importance of honesty.

Him hiding a huge secret all these years didn't cause her to question his lessons. But it did force her to view him differently and, to a lesser degree, herself, as well.

Which brought her right back to her potential pregnancy and the need to buy a home pregnancy test. Perhaps because she lost her mother at a young age, perhaps because she witnessed the miracle of new life on a weekly basis with her job, keeping a baby was the only option for Mel.

Sitting alone on her back patio, watching a glorious sun peeking out from above her neighbors' roofs, Mel couldn't help but feel optimistic. Even if Aaron didn't want their child, her mind and her heart were made up. Granted, there would be obstacles to overcome and challenges to face. But a baby? A beautiful, tiny being brought into this world by her? Mel would fall head over heels at first sight.

She definitely wouldn't fall head over heels for a man who didn't want their child. The next instant, she dismissed the notion. For one, her pregnancy had yet to be confirmed. Two, she had no clue of Aaron's feelings on the subject, since she hadn't told him. Three, he had a daughter whom he adored and cherished. The man was a natural born father. She doubted the accidental circumstances of their child's birth, if there even was a child, would change him.

Before meeting Aaron, Mel had never approached sex casually. She did date, a couple guys semiseriously. Frankie accused her of being afraid to commit, a hang-up from losing their mother. There might be a sliver of truth to that. Mel tended to believe she simply hadn't fallen in love.

After meeting Aaron, she had tried to convince herself she was capable of remaining emotionally uninvolved. How wrong she'd been. Worse, she'd set herself up for being hurt by growing fonder and fonder of a man who couldn't have been clearer about his unavailability.

What should she say to him if she was indeed pregnant? Give him an out? Amicably part ways? Admit the truth about her feelings for him?

She recalled the previous evening when he'd dropped her off and kissed the back of her hand. How sweet was that? And romantic. There was also his kindness toward Samantha—which was touching, and now that Mel wasn't smack-dab in the middle of a tense family discussion, she could admit it.

Oh, Samantha. What to do about her? The

abrupt change in direction her mind took damp-ened Mel's spirits.

Frankie appeared ready to accept the young woman as a member of the family. Then again, Frankie was the motherly type. She'd looked out for Mel and Ronnie after their mother died and, these days, was fiercely protective of her own daughters. She regularly took in stray dogs and cats, finding them good homes and keep-ing them if she couldn't. Ronnie's willingness to help Samantha was likely due to their shared interest in barrel racing.

Mel had decided at some point she'd at least examine the horse. There'd be no harm in it, and the exam would get Frankie off Mel's back. Plus, she was curious about the horse's injury and the prognosis. Beyond that, she'd make no commitment.

Hearing a noise, she turned to see the door leading to the patio open and Dolores step out-side.

"You're up."

"Morning," Mel said. "What brings you by?"

Dolores's appearance wasn't out of the ordinary. Mel and Ronnie had a tendency to leave
their doors unlocked when they were home, a
habit formed from small-town living and family members who frequently dropped by unexpectedly.

"I brought you something." Dolores held up
a small paper sack.

"What's that?"

She came over, sat on the other lounge chair
and passed the sack to Mel. "See for yourself."

Mel sat up, opened the sack, peered in and
read the label on the box. She arched a brow at
her stepmom. "A home pregnancy test?"

"Stopped at the market on my way over."

"Get any snide comments?"

Dolores laughed. "Like I care."

"Thank you."

Mel didn't take Dolores's purchasing the pregnancy test as interfering in something that was
none of her business. She truly appreciated having the older woman's advice and help.

"You could take it now," Dolores suggested.

Mel swallowed, her throat suddenly dry. Now that the moment was upon her, she hesitated. There were so many uncertainties, not the least of which was Aaron's feelings for her.

"The instructions recommend seeing a doctor to verify the results."

Mel glanced up from staring at the package. "You read them?"

"I've taken the test before. Though it's been a long while."

Gathering her courage, Mel rose from the chair and headed into the house, Dolores following close behind.

"Do you want me to stay or leave?"

"Stay," Mel said without reservation. She might need a shoulder to lean on.

In her bedroom, she read and reread the instructions, her anxiety escalating with each paragraph. She was actually doing this, taking a home pregnancy test. Focusing became difficult, and the printing on the leaflet blurred. Finally, when she felt ready, she took the testing wand with her into the adjoining bathroom.

After that, it was a matter of waiting the longest three minutes of her life.

Determined not to peek until the required time had passed, Mel placed the testing wand on the bathroom counter, set the timer on her phone and returned to her bedroom where she proceeded to pace and stare at her phone and struggle to contain her racing thoughts. Finally, three minutes became two, and Mel stared as the numbers changed.

Would Aaron be angry if she was pregnant? She'd assured him she was taking the Pill. What if he thought she'd tricked him?

Mel pressed a palm to her warm cheek, taking another spin around the room. What? Still one minute to go?

Unknotting and reknotting the belt on her bathrobe, she scooped up a pile of dirty laundry she'd left on the floor the previous night and tossed it in the hamper sitting near the bathroom door.

Her gaze went to the testing wand sitting on the counter. Mel swallowed a startled cry. Even from this distance, she could see the results. Lunging forward, she grabbed the wand.

Her spaghetti legs took her only as far as the bed where she plopped down. Her breath came fast, and her heart beat a hundred miles a minute as relief washed over her. Now that the results of the pregnancy test were literally in her hands, she was able to admit what she'd wanted all along but was afraid to say.

A soft knock interrupted her. Dolores stood in the doorway, her expression expectant. "Well?"

Mel waved the wand, happiness filling her as she erupted in a wide grin. "It's positive. I'm pregnant."

Chapter Six

At the kitchen sink, Mel turned on the water and poured the remains of her coffee down the drain. That, she decided, had been her last official taste of caffeine for the next seven-and-a-half months, or thereabouts. She'd learn her exact due date when she saw her doctor, hopefully this week.

Mel wrote herself a note to call him first thing tomorrow morning, not that she'd need reminding. If the doctor was booked and couldn't see her right away, she'd visit the medical clinic in town. Just to verify her pregnancy and obtain prenatal vitamins.

Oddly enough, from the moment she took the test, she'd felt physically fine. Not the least bit nauseous or fatigued. If anything, she was bursting with energy.

"What are you doing?" Dolores asked.

Mel paused from rummaging through the kitchen cupboard. "Looking for the herbal tea Ronnie bought last winter when she had the flu."

"Since when do you drink herbal tea?"

"Since I quit caffeine."

Dolores sat at the kitchen table, texting her oldest son who lived in Louisiana. She also regularly Skyped with her other son and daughter.

Mel had to laugh. Her father barely understood the workings of his phone while Dolores was an expert.

Finding the tea at last, Mel heated a cup in the microwave, then sat down next to her stepmom.

Putting her phone aside, Dolores asked, "Does Aaron know about the baby?"

Mel jerked, almost spilling her tea. "Who told?"

"It's not hard to figure out. You two have been pretty cozy of late."

"What about Dad?"

"Don't worry. I haven't said anything. But he's not stupid. Neither are your sisters."

"I'll tell them. Eventually."

"They've seen you and Aaron being cozy, too. So far, they think you're just flirting."

Mel should've seen this coming, probably had but chose to turn a blind eye.

"I thought you might have told him last night when he took you home," Dolores said.

"My mind was otherwise occupied."

"Be careful you don't wait too long."

"We have tentative plans to talk soon." Mel sipped at her tea, which was more of a distraction than a restorative beverage. "Speaking of Dad, how is he this morning?"

"You could call him."

Mel had considered it earlier then changed her mind. "I'm not ready."

"He's worried about you and your sisters. He's convinced you hate him."

"Of course I don't. But I'm mad and with good reason."

"You're changing the subject," Dolores scolded. "We were discussing you and Aaron and the baby."

"Family first. Aaron next. I can only deal with one problem at a time."

Her stepmom released a heavy sigh. "A huge upheaval isn't what I expected two months into my marriage."

"You knew, didn't you? About Samantha?"

She was slow to respond. "Yes."

"Dammit!" Mel let her hand fall hard to the table. "He told you but not us. That hurts."

"For the record, I disagreed with him. It's the only fight we've ever had. I conceded because the story of Sam was his to tell and didn't directly concern me. But secrets don't generally stay secrets forever, and I worried that you and your sisters would find it hard to forgive him when you did find out. I take no satisfaction in being right."

Mel appreciated the other woman's honesty and that she saw Mel's side. Her father had found a special lady the day he met Dolores, which was, of all places, on an internet dating website for seniors. Mel had been amused by it all, Ronnie, embarrassed. Their father meeting women online! Frankie had been the most encouraging. Similar to how she was the one welcoming Samantha and enlisting the entire family to help her.

When the sisters finally met Dolores, they'd liked her from the start and not only because of her sweet nature and fun personality. Their father had been alone for too many years. Even after the sisters were grown and on their own, he'd remained a bachelor. The only new "ladies" to enter his life were Frankie's daughters.

Mel had quit suggesting he "get out more," or "find someone interesting." Little had she known he'd already done that years ago with Samantha's mother.

"Do you think I'm being unreasonable?"

Mel had asked Aaron the same question last night. As with him, she was genuinely curious in the answer.

Dolores studied her. "You are going to examine Samantha's horse, aren't you?"

"Yeah. I guess."

"Then, no, you're not being unreasonable. As far as being angry at your father, I'd be shocked if you weren't."

"Frankie and Ronnie don't act mad."

"Maybe not on the surface. Underneath, I'd bet they're fuming, too. You and Samantha are the only ones letting your true feelings show, and I say, bully for you."

"What's your opinion of Frankie's plan?"

"When your father won the lottery, I mentioned Samantha and that he might want to consider giving her a small share. He was, and still is, hurt that she refused contact with him when she turned sixteen. I suggested he put a sum aside in a bank account in case he changed his mind later on. He didn't. He was afraid there wouldn't be enough for you girls to get what you wanted and for us to go on an expensive honeymoon."

"Is that really the reason?"

"Who am I to argue?" She shrugged. "The money was his to spend as he wished. Just like telling you about Sam was his story to tell. Not mine."

Sam. Mel had heard her father address Samantha by the nickname last night. Then, like now, a sharp pain pierced her chest right next to her heart.

Francine, Melody and Rhonda. Those were the names appearing on her and her sisters' birth certificates. The shortened, slightly masculine versions, Frankie, Mel and Ronnie, had been bestowed on them by their father. Until last night, Mel had thought that made her and her sisters special. Did he also choose Samantha's name?

Mel swallowed, hoping to dull the pain. "You still didn't tell me what you think of Frankie's plan."

Dolores hesitated. "As long as you're all in agreement, it's a good one."

"Really?"

"Sam's related to us, a part of the family, whether we like it or not and whether we accept it or not."

"That doesn't obligate Frankie, Ronnie and me to give her money we don't have anymore."

"I agree. But if you girls don't agree to help Sam, your dad will have to mortgage the house or cash in some of his retirement."

Mad as Mel was at him, she didn't want him to put a strain on his finances or deplete his 401(k). Dolores had a decent job as an insurance rep and her own retirement account, but she shouldn't have to give Samantha money, either.

"Like Frankie suggested last night, working together to help Sam would be a good way for all of you to get to know her."

Mel looked away. "What if I don't want to get to know her?"

"She's collateral damage," Dolores said, "just like you and your sisters. She didn't ask for what happened to her. Can you imagine being sixteen and finding out the man you thought was your father is, in fact, your adoptive father? That had to be rough."

"What's wrong with her mother anyway? Why doesn't she help Samantha?"

"Maybe she did and the lottery money's just an excuse."

Mel drew back. "For what?"

"Sam could finally be ready to meet you all and wasn't sure how to go about it."

"There are better ways. Like picking up the phone and making a call."

"She's eighteen. Probably not very experienced in handling difficult situations."

Mel made a face. "I think she's spoiled."

"I'm not excusing what she did. Just offering one possible explanation."

"Hmm." Mel would have to ponder that for a little while. "Would I be considered uncooperative if I insisted on a few stipulations before I agree to go along with Frankie's plan?"

"Not by me. What are they?"

"One really. I think we should take this week by week, if not day by day. Should me or anyone want out, we can withdraw with no hard feelings and no scorn from the others."

"You want that in writing?"

Mel laughed. "Not a bad idea. I'll draft a rough agreement."

"Need help?."

"I was kidding."

"I'm not." Dolores shrugged. "You all should at least discuss a flexible set of rules. This isn't easy. I admire you for putting aside your personal feelings."

"No guarantee they'll stay there."

Dolores leaned in closer. "Now, about the baby."

"I'm going to wait to tell Aaron until after I've been to the doctor. Just in case." Sage Powell, Mel's friend and client's wife, had recently miscarried very early in her pregnancy. They were just now trying again.

"You're going to keep the baby then?"

"Absolutely."

"And if Aaron doesn't want another child?"

"I'll let him off the hook."

"Oh, Mel. Is that really wise? Being a single mother is hard. Just ask Frankie. She could really use child support payments, not to mention a helping hand with the girls' care."

Mel reconsidered. "I'll accept Aaron's help if he offers. But I won't force him to take any responsibility. Or acknowledge the baby if he doesn't want to."

"Are you serious? Not acknowledge the baby?" Dolores looked stricken. "In the first place, Mustang Valley is a small town. He's going to run into you and his child. Frequently. In the second place, you can see how that plan didn't work out at all for your father and Sam's mother. He needs to step up, and you need to let him."

"I won't wreck his life."

"Who's to say you would?"

Mel rested her elbow on the table and propped up her chin with her hand. "His wife sacrificed months of her life in order to have their baby. If not a year. He carries a lot of guilt."

"I can imagine."

"He loves Kaylee more than anything and promised Nancy a home with them as long as she wanted one. She'll be devastated when she learns about the baby and think Aaron is betraying her daughter."

"Aaron's still a young man. What is he, thirty-two?

"Thirty-three." Mel would be thirty herself in a few months.

"It's reasonable to expect he'd eventually meet someone new and have more children."

"I don't think Nancy's ready for him to move on, and he's not ready to set wider boundaries or push her away." Mel didn't like the hoarse quality in her voice. "She's your friend. Is she as needy as she appears?"

"She does rely on Kaylee and Aaron to fill the void Robin left. Obviously, too much."

"Yet another reason for me not to pressure him."

"That doesn't change the responsibility he has to you and the baby," Dolores insisted. "Think hard before you let him off the hook."

"This wasn't his fault."

"Or yours. It takes two to make a baby."

Mel didn't answer.

"Have faith in him. He deserves a chance."

Whether intentional or not, Dolores had hit the nail on the head. Mel's nagging doubts didn't allow her to believe in a possible future with Aaron. "I'm the one who insisted on a no-strings-attached relationship. He's playing entirely by my rules."

"Which you now regret."

"Only because I'm pregnant."

Dolores smiled. "Only because you're falling for him."

Mel's shoulders sagged. "So much for modern relationships. They're apparently not for me."

Her cell phone rang. She pushed back from the table and hurried to the bedroom to answer it before the call went to voice mail. She got there just in time.

Seeing the familiar number, she answered with a breathy, "Hello, Cara."

"Sorry to bother you on a Sunday morning."

"No problem. Is something wrong?"

Cara Dempsey was the owner and manager of the mustang sanctuary, a local refuge for neglected, displaced and unadoptable mustangs. There were usually two hundred or more formerly wild mustangs residing in the sanctuary at any given time. Mel made regular trips, donating her services. When forced to charge, she always gave Cara and the sanctuary a deep discount.

"We had five head go missing last night," Cara said. "From the maternity pasture."

"Oh, my God!" Another horse theft. Less than a week after the last one. "Did you call the authorities?"

"Yes. Right away." Cara sobbed. "Four of the mares were pregnant. The fifth was a new mother. Her foal is three weeks old. I'm worried about the little guy. I tried bottle-feeding him, but he refuses."

Mel felt a tug on her heart. Losing a foal was always devastating. Losing one who wasted away because it missed its mother, even worse.

"If you don't have an empty stall in the horse stables, clear one and put him there. I'll meet you in an hour."

As soon as Dolores heard about the call, she left, promising to update Mel's dad on the horse theft. He'd probably want to head to The Small Change where the sanctuary was located even though it technically wasn't his responsibility.

Mel showered and dressed in record time, mentally inventorying what supplies she'd need to care for the foal and which techniques she'd employ to encourage it to eat.

Going outside to inspect her truck, she swore when she discovered she was low on mare's formula. Once on the road, she called the owner of Mustang Valley Feed and Supply Depot. Normally, the store wasn't open on Sundays, but the owner made an exception and promised Mel that his niece and assistant manager would meet her there.

She hung up, refusing to let herself wonder if Aaron would be at The Small Change when she arrived, investigating the horse theft—and hoping he'd be there just the same.

"I WANNA COME with you, Daddy." Kaylee peered up at Aaron, her huge blue eyes, so like her mother's, pleading with him.

"Sorry, sweetie." It tore at him, having to leave her again, especially after he'd gotten home too late last night to read to her.

"I don't understand why you have to go out again," Nancy said.

She and Kaylee were lingering over Sunday breakfast. That had been Aaron's plan as well, along with taking Kaylee to the park in town before it got too hot outside. Those plans went by the wayside twenty minutes ago, when he received a call about a horse theft at the mustang sanctuary.

Normally, he might let Shonda, the deputy on duty, handle things on her own. But she was new to the job and a rookie to boot. On top of that, she didn't have a lot of experience with livestock, none before taking this job. Eduardo, the other deputy, had requested the day off to visit his ailing grandmother in Apache Junction and wasn't available. That left only Aaron.

"I won't be long. I'm just checking on Shonda. Ninety minutes tops." He lifted his hand and smoothed Kaylee's curls, also just like her mother's. "We'll go to the park when I get back."

Nancy made the pinched face she always did when Aaron disappointed her or his daughter. "It'll be a hundred degrees by then."

"How about I take the two of you to the new aquarium and butterfly exhibit?" He'd been saving that trip for Kaylee's third birthday next month. Now, he'd have to come up with something else.

"Yay!" Kaylee bounced in her chair.

"You spoil her too much," Nancy admonished.

"And you don't?" Aaron grinned good-naturedly, attempting to lighten his mother-in-law's mood.

"That's a grandmother's prerogative." Her

features softened as they always did when she looked at Kaylee. "But we'll let you off the hook this time."

Aaron hadn't expected anything less. One thing he and Nancy had in common was spoiling Kaylee whenever possible.

A kiss and hug for Kaylee, a goodbye to Nancy and Aaron was out the door and on his way to the mustang sanctuary. Radioing Shonda, he learned the deputy was with Cara Dempsey in the ranch office housed in a building adjacent to the horse stables.

The Small Change Ranch, home to the sanctuary, was one of the larger cattle operations in the valley, running over two thousand head. Advances in technology during the last fifty years had impacted how cattle were raised. One aspect, however, remained the same. Ranch hands still utilized horses for much of the work. In addition to the various barns, The Small Change boasted a state-of-the-art, air-conditioned horse stable and numerous pastures, including the one exclusive to pregnant and nursing mares, and where the latest horse theft had occurred.

Aaron aimed his SUV in the direction of the ranch office. Spying Mel's pickup parked in front of the stables, he executed a sharp right. Shonda and Cara could wait a few more minutes. Having discovered Mel at the ranch changed his priorities.

He spotted her immediately upon entering the stables. She stood in a horse stall, the sixth from the end, her back to him and bent over something. He started to call her name, only to reconsider and instead walk quietly down the aisle.

She was holding a bottle to a young foal's mouth and encouraging him to drink. At her feet sat a black rubber bucket and her medical case. The foal didn't act interested in the bottle and kept trying to pull away, bobbing his head vigorously. Mel made escape difficult by locking one arm around the foal's neck and putting herself between him and the stall door.

"Come on," she cooed, pushing the nipple into

the foal's mouth. "You can do this. Aren't you even a little hungry?"

The foal abruptly jerked and almost broke free.

"Pretty please?" Her voice had become strained. "You need fluids or you'll get dehydrated. We can't let that happen. Trust me, the outcome isn't good."

Aaron watched Mel, unable to take his eyes off her. He'd seen her treat animals before, that was nothing out of the ordinary, and witnessed the enormity of her caring. Never had he seen her with such a young patient or sensed her deep emotional involvement.

Veterinary medicine wasn't just a job to her. It was her way of making the world a tiny bit better for everyone else. Kind of like how law enforcement wasn't just a job to him.

The revelation gave Aaron pause. He and Mel were more alike than he'd realized.

With each jerk of the foal's head, Mel's long braid swayed like a pendulum. He liked her no fuss hairstyle and thought it suited her. He liked better undoing her braid and running his fingers through the long blond strands, marveling at their glossy sheen.

From this angle, her shapely curves were accentuated and inspired thoughts having nothing to do with work and everything to do with stolen hours alone together in the dark. He pictured her head fitting perfectly into the crook of his shoulder when they snuggled as if their bodies were custom-made for just that purpose.

The twinge of guilt came right on schedule. Not so much from his thoughts dishonoring Robin's memory but from disregarding the promise he'd made to put Kaylee and his family first.

All at once, Mel glanced up and, for a moment, they stared at each other. Aaron because he liked looking at her. A lot.

"I didn't expect to see you today," she finally said, shaking off the spell they were under.

"I thought your deputy was investigating the horse theft."

"I'm backing her up."

The foal suddenly slipped from Mel's grasp and scurried to the far corner of the stall. She didn't go after him. Setting the bottle down, she rubbed the small of her back, which had to ache from maintaining such an awkward position.

"She's in the ranch office talking to Cara, if you're looking for her."

"I know." Aaron closed the distance to the stall and leaned a forearm on the door. "I talked to her earlier."

"Then why are you here?" She looked around, indicating the horse stables.

He grinned. "To see you. And I'm glad I did."

She actually glanced shyly away. In that instant, he became even more smitten—which meant he was treading further and further into forbidden territory.

To distract himself, Aaron nodded at the foal. With a coat the color of tarnished gold, a wide white blaze down the center of his face and four perfectly matched white stockings, he was striking to say the least. "That's a nice looking colt. What happened to the mother? Is she sick?"

"She's gone. She's one of the missing horses." Aaron swore softly, cursing the horse thieves.

"I'm worried we're going to lose him." Mel sighed wearily. "He won't eat."

"You'll figure this out. He's not going to die."

"No, he's not." She straightened. "I still have a trick or two up my sleeve."

"Like what?" He was truly interested. Aaron had grown up around horses, though his family hadn't raised any from birth.

"There's milk pellets. According to Cara, he's been eating a little solid food. But he's still going to need the complete nutrition of mare's milk. I checked around, and there aren't any lactating mares available to foster him. But there are several tame burros in the sanctuary that could serve as a companion. A large part of this guy's problem is he misses his mother. His chances of improving increase if he can bond with another horse. Or something close to a horse."

"If you want some help," he said, "let me know."

She searched his face. "Seriously?"

"I wouldn't have offered if I wasn't serious."

"Thank you."

Aaron had to look twice. Were those tears in her eyes? "It's no big deal. Really."

"What's your mother-in-law going to say if we're seen together?"

"I'd like to say I don't care."

"Except you do." Mel wiped off the bottle with a towel and returned it to her medical case.

"Helping you with the foal is business. Not personal."

"Of course. So why would Nancy care?"

"Okay." Aaron could have kicked himself. "That didn't come out right."

"You think?" Mel's movements were stiff and jerky as she collected the bucket and closed her medical case.

"I'm sorry."

She nodded, her mouth drawn into a thin, tight line. "I put you on the spot. That wasn't fair."

Aaron should probably leave before he shoved his other foot in his mouth. Only he didn't. "Things settle down with the family yet?"

Her answer came slowly. "I haven't talked to my dad or sisters since last night. And before you say anything, I will. I needed to handle this emergency first."

"You consider Frankie's plan at all?"

"And some other things." She pushed her hair back from her face. "I didn't sleep much last night."

He just then noticed the dark circles beneath her eyes and reached for her across the stall door. Too quick for him, she retreated a step, her no-touching message broadcasted loud and clear.

Should he tell her he was finding it harder and harder to resist her? Probably not. She'd been the one to set the rules, it was true, but he'd agreed to them, as much for his personal situation as hers.

Robin had made him swear he'd be open to finding someone new someday. At the time, when she'd been lying in a hospital bed, he couldn't conceive of loving again. Lately, with Mel, the prospects didn't seem completely impossible.

The pull between them was definitely growing stronger and stronger. But his home life, of which Nancy was a big part, remained unchanged. He'd made commitments to her, too, and Aaron didn't like going back on his word. Even something as small as missing reading time with Kaylee bothered him.

"You're an easy person to like, Mel." It was the closest he could come to expressing his feelings.

She stared, her features stricken.

Aaron wanted to kick himself. Once again, his remark had hurt her rather than ease her unhappiness or uncertainty.

"Let's meet tonight." At her arch glance, he added, "For that talk. Nothing else."

After a moment, she relented. "Is six o'clock too early?"

"Can we make it seven? I'm taking Kaylee to that new aquarium and butterfly exhibit this afternoon."

The briefest of smiles touched Mel's face. "That should be fun."

Aaron thought it might be more fun if Mel went with them. He didn't dare ask her, though. That was guaranteed to make a muddy situation muddier. He set the fantasy aside, along with the other ones he'd recently been having about him and Mel going to dinner and a movie rather than hiding out in a room at the motel.

"I'd better head to the office. Check in with Shonda and see how the investigation is progressing."

"And I need to track down a good companion burro."

Mel bent to retrieve her case, then abruptly straightened, her hand clasped to her middle, her eyes squeezed shut and her lower lip caught between her teeth.

"You okay?" Aaron pushed through the stall door.

She held up a hand. "Stay back."

Ignoring her, he hurried to her side.

"Please." She spun sideways. "I'm going to be sick."

She barely made it to the corner opposite where the foal stood watching them with wide eyes before leaning over and vomiting.

Aaron waited a minute for her to recover. She was breathing hard, as if she'd just run a hundred-yard dash. Averting her head, she wiped her mouth with her forearm, kicking dirt to cover the mess at her feet.

Her acute embarrassment tangible, he said, "Don't worry. I have a young daughter. I see throw up and a whole lot worse on a regular basis."

She exhaled slowly. Sweat lined her brow, from the heat and the exertion. "You haven't seen my throw up."

"You should call your doctor. This has been going on for days."

"I'm planning on it. Tomorrow."

"I could drive you."

What little color remained in her cheeks promptly drained. "No, that's all right. I can manage."

Before he could say more, she doubled over and vomited again. This, he decided, was getting serious.

"Go home, Mel. Forget about the burro. You're sick."

"No, I'm not." She wiped at her mouth again.

"Do I have to toss you over my shoulder and kidnap you?"

"You'd better be joking."

"I'm not, Mel. You're really worrying me."

Drawing in a long breath, she blurted, "I'm pregnant. I was going to tell you tonight, but there's no point in waiting."

Pregnant? Aaron struggled to absorb the news, but his mind kept throwing up barriers.

"You're…on the Pill," he stammered.

"It obviously failed."

Her tone implied she was mad, though Aaron wasn't sure at what. Him or the situation.

A beep, a crackle and then a distorted version of Shonda's voice erupted from his radio. "Aaron. Are you here yet? We're waiting on you. Over."

He responded automatically, pressing the button on the transmitter clipped to his shirtfront. "Be right there."

To Mel, he said, "I don't want to go."

"I understand. You're here on official business. I should have waited to tell you."

"I don't know how long I'll be tied up with the investigation. Then I have plans with Kaylee. Can this wait until tonight?"

"Sure." She stared at him. If she was attempting to gauge his reaction, he didn't think she was getting much other than surprise and disbelief.

What did she expect? She had just pulled the rug out from under him.

He knew he should reassure her. Tell her everything would be okay. That they'd figure this out, and she could rely on him.

All he could muster at the moment was, "All right. See you then."

He could only guess at the depths of her disappointment in him.

Chapter Seven

Mel waited until she reached the four-way stop before grabbing her phone off the passenger seat and reading the text. It was from Aaron, as she'd suspected.

#22 Be there shortly

He was giving her the number for their room at the Desert Oasis Motel. This was the extent of their texts, a room number and a few token words.

Returning her phone to the passenger seat, she accelerated though the quiet rural intersection and continued on the road toward Rio Verde. For some ridiculous reason, she thought Aaron might say something different tonight. Like, *hurry up, can't wait to see you* or *I've missed you* followed by a heart emoji.

She was being stupid. Ten hours ago she'd delivered the bombshell of the century. Did she really think the subtle changes she'd noticed in him lately would carry over to a text when he was probably still reeling?

Neither would tonight be a typical hookup. No falling into bed after a few minutes of small talk.

On the plus side, her morning sickness had all but disappeared since this morning's disastrous encounter in the horse stall.

An hour researching online, as well as reading pamphlets a nurse at the medical clinic had provided that afternoon, had taught Mel this particular pregnancy symptom often came and went. With luck, her stomach would behave. Hard to have a conversation when one person was bent over the toilet.

She didn't return Aaron's text and not because it was unsafe to do so while driving. She simply didn't know what to say. Her usual reply of *On my way* seemed trite under the circumstances.

Aaron's SUV was easy to spot in the small parking area behind the motel. He hadn't driven his official sheriff's department vehicle. Too risky. What if someone spotted him? Rather, he drove his personal SUV, a smaller, "friendlier" and completely unremarkable version that garnered no attention.

Mel parked in the next space over, noting the child's car seat through the window. She was struck with a sudden pang. Would he have a second car seat for their baby? Or, not want anything to do with Mel anymore?

Her father had given up all parental rights to Samantha without a single objection. Aaron could easily want that too. He already had a family, one he'd sacrificed a great deal for. A baby and baby mama on the side could endanger their security.

A heavy lump formed in the pit of her stomach that had nothing to do with the physical aspects of her pregnancy and everything to do with her emotional state. She could well be facing motherhood alone. Not the future she'd envisioned for herself.

Standing in front of the door to room 22, she raised her hand to knock, then paused, a sense of indecency heating her cheeks. She hadn't been embarrassed since the first time she and Aaron came here. They'd met in the lobby, and she'd been convinced the clerk pegged them right off the bat as having an affair.

By their third rendezvous at the motel, Mel hadn't cared about proprieties. She and Aaron weren't doing anything wrong. So why, then, had those old feelings suddenly resurfaced?

She fought the urge to turn and flee. Aaron was expecting her. And besides, they really did need to talk.

Rapping soundly on the door, she waited, every nerve in her body stretched to its limit. He answered almost immediately, as if he'd been standing directly on the other side of the door.

"Hi." The smile he flashed paled in comparison to its usual brilliance.

Mel worried it was a bad sign. "Sorry I'm late."

She entered the room when he swung the door wide and gave a cursory glance around. The two dozen rooms at the small motel were identically furnished and decorated. Realizing she and Aaron had occupied over half of them, she nearly laughed. From tension, not because she found the idea funny.

He didn't pull her into a hug or kiss her, which was how most of their evenings together started and ended. It was a definite highlight of their time together and one she usually looked forward to.

"You want some water?" He came prepared with two chilled bottles, which now sat on the spindly legged desk.

"Thanks." She might need an outlet for her pent-up energy. Sipping water would serve the purpose.

After a moment, he planted himself in the

equally spindly chair, his long jeans-clad legs fighting for space in the cramped area between the desk and the bed. "How's the foal doing?"

Apparently, they *were* going to start with small talk.

"Putting the burro in with him hasn't helped." She sighed dejectedly. "He did finally drink milk from a bucket and nibbled on a few pellets."

"You think he'll make it?"

"Too early to say. The next few days, few hours, really, are critical. Cara's keeping an eye on him."

"You'll pull him through."

Aaron had said something similar to her this morning, and it pleased her that his confidence hadn't wavered in light of recent events.

"I hope."

Silence followed. Sipping at her water, Mel perched on the bed. The mattress, as hard as an ironing board, barely budged. On past evenings, when their moods were lighter, they'd joked about the motel's lousy accommodations.

"Who wants to start?" she asked, forcing a smile.

"How about you, seeing as you have the most at stake?"

Did she? Mel tended to disagree. Unless he *was* planning on leaving her to raise the baby alone.

"I went to the medical clinic in town today and had the pregnancy confirmed." Since early pregnancy tests could be wrong, and there was a lot riding on their talk tonight, she'd decided to make absolutely sure by visiting the clinic. "I'm calling my regular doctor tomorrow for an appointment."

"Want me to drive you?"

His offer initially took her aback. She hadn't thought about him going with her. Then again, he'd probably accompanied his late wife on all her appointments, considering she'd spent the majority of her pregnancy battling a brain tumor.

"That's not necessary," Mel said. "Maybe when I'm further along."

"How far are you?"

"Five weeks, give or take." She hesitated, her certainty waning. "You do believe me when I say this was entirely an accident?"

"Of course."

"Really?" Doubts still plagued her.

"Mel, I know you pretty well. We've been seeing each other for over eight months. You're not a liar. The Pill can fail. It did with Robin."

"Oh!" He hadn't mentioned that before. "I always had the impression you and she were trying for a baby."

"We were when we had Kaylee. The year before, Robin conceived while on the Pill. Unfortunately, she miscarried. I always wondered if she was so determined to have Kaylee because she'd lost one baby."

Mel had no idea what she would do if she were terminally ill. Maybe the same as Robin. Oddly enough, the thought made her feel a tiny connection to Aaron's late wife. While disconcerting, it was also comforting in a way.

"Since this wasn't what either of us planned,"

Mel began, "I completely understand if you want no part of the baby."

He stared at her. "You're kidding."

"Actually, no."

"I'm the baby's father, Mel. Trust me, I'll be an involved father."

He sounded completely committed. Not a trace of hesitancy or uncertainty colored his voice.

Mel wanted to be glad. Relieved. Aaron was willing to step up. But something held her back.

"I just wanted to put it out there. I have no expectations."

"You should," he said. "High expectations. And I promise to meet them. I was thrown today when you told me, and I apologize for that. Please don't think too badly of me."

"I didn't. Honestly. You were caught off guard."

"It was a lot to process. But I've been thinking about you, about us, all day."

As she looked at him, her hesitancy wavered. Aaron was the kind of man Mel had always dreamed of meeting—someday, when she was ready to settle down. His intentions were clearly good.

"I suppose we have a decision or two to make."

"Let's not try to figure everything out tonight," he said. "We have time."

She thought it interesting that he hadn't asked her if she wanted the baby or not. Had he assumed or—and this was irksome if true—did he know her as well as he'd claimed?

"I'm going to support you," he continued, "financially and in every way you need."

"What about your family? Will you tell them?"

"Yes. Eventually."

She supposed Aaron had a valid reason to wait. She wasn't very far along and, as she'd learned tonight, his late wife had miscarried.

"What about you?" he asked. "Telling anyone?"

"Dolores knows, but only because she found me being sick in the café restroom and figured it out. But she won't say anything until I'm ready."

"You sure? Not even your dad?"

"I trust Dolores."

"That says a lot about her character. You must be close."

His remark prompted Mel to stop and think. "I guess we are."

"I'm glad. You can use a friend right now. Someone besides me."

Mel studied him, noting the rugged good looks and strong physique that had first attracted her. He appeared capable of taking down the burliest of criminal offenders. Yet, she'd seen his gentler side many times, with her and, from a distance, with his daughter.

"Are you my friend, Aaron?"

"I'd like to think so." He sat up, causing the old chair to creak. "More, if you'll let me."

What was he implying?

Nothing, apparently, for he continued with, "We're having a baby together. Better for everyone involved if we get along."

"Yeah. Right." She sighed. "How is Nancy going to take the news?"

"Honestly?" he asked.

"That's the only answer I'm interested in."

"Probably not great."

While putting her vet practice first had been Mel's reason for keeping their relationship status casual, Nancy's hold on Aaron was the driving force behind his. Mel disliked being harsh. He had lost the woman he loved. But it was as if Nancy didn't want him moving on. She fanned his guilt over Robin's death, keeping the flame alive and burning bright.

"She has to expect you're going to meet someone eventually." For a moment, Mel thought Aaron might confess that he already had. It didn't happen.

"She's been good to me and Kaylee since Robin died."

Mel didn't press the issue. She had no right. He was entitled to tell Nancy in his own time and in his own way.

"What about you?" Aaron asked. "Not your family but your job. Having a baby is going to interfere in a big way with your work schedule."

"You're right. I'll have to make some changes. But other single mothers manage." She was thinking of her older sister. "I will, too."

"No rush. You have a lot on your plate at the moment."

He didn't ask the obvious question, for which she was glad. How did she expect to simultaneously build her practice and raise a child? Perhaps he, like Mel, believed she didn't have to choose and could succeed at both.

"I want this baby," she said, admitting out loud what was in her heart.

His response was an ear-to-ear grin. "I can tell. I'm excited, too."

"You are?"

"It was hard being happy when Kaylee was born. Don't get me wrong, I wanted her. But I was losing Robin. She was dying by degrees, and each day was a challenge. This time, with you, I can celebrate. Pass out cigars. Laugh when the guys make jokes."

His admission struck a tender chord in Mel's heart. If she hadn't thought him perfect before, she did now. Managing to keep her distance was getting harder and harder.

They spent the next thirty minutes discussing less pressing matters. It seemed not all of Aaron's memories of Robin's pregnancy were sad. He had some humorous and sweet stories to tell, too.

Any other night, they would have made love. Tonight, however, they were there to talk, and it was Aaron who suggested they get a move on as they both had early mornings.

He walked with her to her truck. "Good night, Mel. Drive safely."

"You, too. I'll let you know about the doctor's appointment."

Assuming a parting kiss was unlikely, she reached for her door handle—and was caught off guard when his arm captured her by the waist.

"Aaron! What—"

He lifted her off her feet and hard against him.

"Is this a good idea?" Her voice wavered. The message earlier had been hands-off.

"You can tell me no." He lowered his mouth, stopping a millimeter shy of kissing her. "Otherwise, hang on."

Hang on? Like to his shoulders? Weak in the knees, she decided maybe she'd better. Just as a precaution.

In the deepest recesses of her mind, a small voice shouted a warning to be careful. This was inviting danger.

She didn't listen. Aaron smelled too delicious and felt too good for her to stop now.

"I've missed you, Mel." He brushed his lips across hers, their touch softer than a butterfly's wings.

The words she'd longed to hear. Aaron had never said them before, in this or any context. Missing her implied he thought about her when they were apart. Hadn't she just ripped the rug out from under him with her pregnancy announcement? Yet, he admitted to missing her.

This wasn't just a matter of growing feelings. There had to be more.

Any other thoughts, coherent or scattered or

wildly improbable, were banished when Aaron's mouth covered hers. He didn't have to demand a response from her, she willingly offered. Clutching the fabric of his shirt in her fingers, she dragged him backward until they stumbled into her truck, and she was pinned between two hard and unyielding surfaces.

Yes. At last. This was what she'd been wanting, needing, craving all night. Letting go and throwing caution to the wind, she lost herself in the kiss.

Wait—that wasn't it at all. She *found* herself. And she wanted to stay. Indefinitely.

Eventually, and too soon for her liking, they slowly broke apart. Just as well. They might have gone a little too far. Their immediate future was up in the air still, and intimacy tended to confuse situations.

But when Mel peered up at Aaron, he wore a grin. Not a satisfied one and not a sexy one. It was…happy. How was that possible when they'd just made a big mistake?

"I'd better go," he said, as reluctant to release her as he'd been to end their kiss.

Rendered speechless, Mel could only nod. With a last, lovely caress to her cheek, he walked away. She stared after him for several seconds before climbing into her truck and starting the engine.

At the first stop, Mel touched a hand to her cheek and then a finger to her lips, reliving the sensation of Aaron's hand and mouth. Unless she was mistaken, he had kissed her as if he wanted her with every fiber of his being. And she had wanted him with the same intensity.

Wrong and dangerous as it was, she hoped they'd make another mistake again soon.

MEL COMMENDED HERSELF for arriving at Frankie's house only—she checked the dash clock—thirty-six minutes late. It had been a crazy busy day with two unscheduled emergencies. Thirty-six minutes late was a pretty impressive accomplishment in her opinion.

Four days had passed since she and Aaron

met up at the motel and shared their incredible kiss. Four days when Mel had a thousand and one important things to contemplate—like her pregnancy and the doctor visit, which had gone well. Aaron telling his mother-in-law and her reaction. Mel telling her family. The latest developments with Samantha.

Yet, unbelievably, Mel was most occupied with the kiss, constantly reliving every vivid detail and analyzing every tiny aspect from beginning to end. It probably meant nothing. She and Aaron had often kissed. No reason to go overboard just because her toes continued to tingle even now.

Her phone beeped, alerting her to a text message. Mel quit breathing. Was it Aaron? They'd been communicating daily, mostly about how she felt, the results of her doctor visit, the young foal's condition and what, if any, progress had been made on the horse thefts. But it was always by phone call. Their last text had been the one on Sunday containing the inn room number.

She checked, saw Frankie's name and told

herself she was glad. Talking to Aaron would only confuse her more.

Frankie's text asked how much longer Mel was going to be. Apparently, her older sister didn't look out her front window much or she'd see Mel's truck sitting there. Then again, she might be in the backyard with Samantha.

Mel answered "Here," then retrieved her medical case from the locked compartment. As expected, Frankie and Samantha were with Mel's newest patient—Samantha's horse.

Entering through the side gate, Mel crossed the large, grassy backyard. Frankie had purchased the country-style house, with its half-acre corral and minibarn especially for her daughters. She'd yet to acquire a pony or small horse for them, still in the process of getting settled after the move. Which meant that Samantha's horse, a long-legged, muscular brown and white paint, had the place to himself.

Judging from his loose-limbed stance and idly swishing tail, he liked his new surroundings.

Same for his owner. Samantha chatted amiably with Frankie, the defiance in her eyes absent for once.

"There you are." Frankie spotted Mel and threw her arms up in exasperation. "Finally. It's after three."

Samantha didn't issue a greeting. She stood beside her horse, perhaps shielding him from danger or taking comfort from him. Mel wasn't sure which. Big John, his lead rope dangling from the fence, shook his head in annoyance at the dozen pesky flies attempting to land.

Mel hadn't changed her opinion of the horse's condition; it would require months of rest and physical therapy for a full recovery. But she did believe he'd eventually compete again and had told Samantha as much.

That, and Ronnie allowing Samantha to use her expensive barrel-racing horse, were likely responsible for the young woman's improved attitude. And possibly Frankie's mothering too. She did have the magic touch.

"Jeez, Mom," Mel teased, "I'm not that late."

She set her case down near the horse and opened
it, revealing an assortment of equipment and
supplies.

Frankie's daughters played nearby, wearing bathing suits and darting in and out of the
water sprinkler. They were having so much fun,
laughing and squealing, they hadn't seen Mel.

She wiped sweat off her forehead with the
back of her hand. Tempted to join her nieces
in the water, she asked Samantha, "How's he
doing today?"

"No better."

"Rehabilitation takes time. You have to be
patient."

"I'm walking him twice a day like you said."

"That's good." Mel conducted her examina-
tion, quizzing Samantha about the horse and
his symptoms.

"And I'm taking him to Powell Ranch tomorrow to work him in the round pen there."

"Don't they usually charge for that?"

Powell Ranch, where Ronnie had her barrel-
racing school, offered several levels of service

to their customers. Mel doubted Samantha could afford the most basic one.

"They're letting me use some of the facilities in exchange for cleaning stalls and exercising horses."

"It was Ronnie's idea," Frankie interjected. "That way, Samantha can train with Ronnie's other students."

Training under Ronnie's supervision. Using her best horse. Living with Frankie. Helping with chores and babysitting her daughters.

Mel marveled at how both her sisters had so readily accepted Samantha. Unless they were just making the best of the situation, which was what Aaron had suggested when they spoke yesterday.

"That's great." Mel was slow to respond.

"She registered for the barrel-racing competition this weekend in Rio Verde," Frankie said.

Mel had heard. Like with bull riding, bronc busting and calf roping, barrel racers often organized nonsanctioned events in order that both the riders and horses could practice as much as possible.

"Dad's driving her." Frankie looked pleased. "And covering the entry fees. We're all going."

Mel continued manipulating Big John's injured leg, gauging his sensitivity to pain. "We?"

"The girls and me. Dad. Dolores. Ronnie, naturally. And you?" she added with a hopeful smile.

"I'm working."

"All day? It doesn't start till early evening."

"She doesn't have to go," Samantha said sulkily.

Mel stifled her temper, irked at being made to feel guilty. "I'll do my best."

One of the girls squealed in anger and took a swing at her sister, fortunately missing by a good foot. Something must have gone wrong during their playing. Frankie rushed over to separate them and make peace.

Mel noticed Samantha watching, a tender expression on her face as if she actually cared about the girls. Who, now that Mel thought about it, were Samantha's nieces. Mel remembered the mention of two younger brothers. Did Samantha miss them? They must be older than the girls.

The next moment, Samantha returned her attention to Big John. Ignoring Mel, she rubbed the broad space between his eyes and cooed softly. Big John responded by lowering his head, pressing his nose into her arm and blowing contentedly.

Liking young children. Loving her horse. Samantha apparently possessed a gentler side. Mel had been like that when she was younger.

That wasn't the only similarity she'd observed between the two of them. Though, to Mel's dismay, she might have more in common with Samantha's mother Carrie Anne. Both had unexpectedly gotten pregnant by a man who still grieved his late wife, and both were reluctant to commit to that man.

Mel reached into her medical case for liniment and leg wraps. Bandaging Big John's leg protected it from further injury, and the liniment improved flexibility. Mel was trying many different methods to help the horse, including exercising and stretches designed to strengthen his leg.

"Can I help?" Samantha asked.

"Um, sure." Mel pointed. "Hand me that square of cotton padding.

Samantha did as instructed and then watched Mel closely as if trying to absorb everything she did.

"You interested in veterinary medicine?"

"I'm interested in taking care of Big John," she answered.

Good enough, thought Mel. "He's a nice horse. Strong. Spirited. Clearly attached to you. I can see why you're upset he's hurt."

"He's all I've got." Samantha continued to stroke the horse's broad face. "I'd do anything for him."

Like demand money from a biological father she hadn't met before?

"What about your family in Flagstaff?"

Samantha didn't answer. Okay, apparently,

Aaron was right. She was on the outs with her parents. Maybe they didn't approve of her choices or disliked her boyfriend. What eighteen-year-old wasn't on the outs with his or her parents at some time?

"I'm really grateful to Ronnie and Frankie." After a long pause, Samantha said, "And you."

Mel almost laughed. "That wasn't so hard, was it?"

Samantha became suddenly preoccupied with Big John. Mel let her be, focusing instead on the horse's leg. Overall, she was satisfied with his improvement, slow though it was.

"Rodeoing is my only shot to make anything of myself."

Mel glanced over her shoulder at Samantha. "I doubt that. You're smart. And pretty capable from what I've seen, no insult intended. I'm sure you have more than one shot. What about college?"

"I'm not going. I don't care what my parents say."

Ah. School was the reason for the falling out.

Had they talked since Samantha came to Mustang Valley? Samantha hadn't taken the news of her mother's lies well. Their original rift could have possibly, and understandably, widened.

"I loved college," Mel said, choosing not to ask about Samantha's mother. "But it's not for everyone. Given the choice, what would you do?"

"Barrel race. What I'm doing now."

Ronnie had made a career of rodeoing. It could be done.

"You'll have to work really hard."

"I'm tough."

This time, Mel did laugh. "No kidding."

Did she actually admire the young woman? When had that happened? Must be her maternal instincts kicking in, messing with her thinking.

"Look, I know you're mad at me…" Samantha stopped there, leaving the sentence unfinished.

"I am." Mel stood. "What you did wasn't right. Demanding money." She braced her hands on her hips. "But, you were lied to by your parents, and, trust me, I understand how you feel."

She had yet to look her father in the eyes since learning his giant secret. "And because my sisters believe you deserve a break, I'm willing to help."

"Okay."

"Okay?" Mel waited.

"Thank you."

A little better. She had no idea why, but she said, "If you'd like to come with me sometime on a call, I wouldn't object. I'm going to need a hand in the coming weeks. With some of the heavier work."

"Help you?" Samantha brightened. "You're offering me a job?"

"No. I can't afford to pay you. Consider it a trade for treating Big John."

Her enthusiasm didn't wane. "When? Tomorrow?"

"Don't you have to watch the girls and train with Ronnie?"

"Frankie doesn't go in to work until noon, and practice starts at 7:00—p.m.," she clarified.

"I'll be by at 6:00 to pick you up—a.m."

Samantha didn't say much else, but Mel caught her smiling to herself and almost tripped on her case. While not a carbon copy, Samantha did have many of the Hartman characteristics, reminding Mel of Ronnie when she was younger. Or, she swallowed, herself.

How could she have missed the resemblance?

"That was nice of you." Frankie had snuck up behind Mel.

"I'm probably going to regret it."

"No, you're not."

They both turned when Aaron's family SUV pulled into the driveway. Mel's heart rate immediately skyrocketed. What was he doing here? He must have spotted her truck while driving by and stopped to talk. She finger combed her hair, scolded herself for caring and let her hand drop.

"Ah!" Frankie said. "Right on time."

"What?" Mel blinked.

"Aaron. He brought Kaylee over for dinner and a playdate with the girls."

Really? They'd just talked a couple hours ago,

and he hadn't mentioned a playdate. Not that he was required to inform her of his schedule. But he'd known she was going to be here.

"What's wrong with you?" Squinting, Frankie shielded her eyes from the sun. "You look funny."

"Nothing." Mel turned away.

Childish though it might be, she was a bit hurt. Aaron hadn't dropped by to see her but rather her sister and nieces. Apparently, she was the only one affected by their kiss.

Chapter Eight

"Wait." Aaron sprinted toward Mel. "Put that down. Better yet, give it to me." He relieved her of the bucket of water, ignoring her protest. "It's too heavy for you."

"I'm not frail and helpless."

"You need to be careful. Don't take any chances. It's hot as blue blazes out here."

"And you're overreacting."

He was, he'd admit to it. "Comes with the territory. I worried a lot about…" He stopped, closed his mouth and started again. "You have to be careful during the first few months."

She turned, her gaze roving his face. He expected her to snap at him. Instead, she said, "That's sweet."

Mel never failed to amaze him. "So, I didn't mess up?"

"You're bound to compare my pregnancy to Robin's. You wouldn't be human if you didn't." The barest of smiles appeared.

Aaron thought about kissing her, a frequent preoccupation lately. First thing in the morning, last thing at night, during work, while pumping gas, images assailed him. He used to look forward to their get-togethers. Now, all he thought about was the last time they'd made love and how much he missed her.

"Who do you compare me to, Mel?"

She had mentioned a few past boyfriends. None that had seemed serious or lasted for more than a year.

"No one. My problem, lately anyway, is comparing you and me to other people."

"Who?" He was curious.

"I hate to admit this." She winced and drew in a breath. "My dad and Samantha's mom."

"Huh." He could see how she'd come to that conclusion.

"Yeah, I feel the same way. Unsettling, isn't it?"

Aaron set down the bucket. This would require some mulling over.

The girls squealing and giggling a short distance away had him glancing around for Kaylee. He should be checking on her, not leave her supervision entirely up to Frankie. Bad parenting on his part. Then again, the second Kaylee had seen her little friends darting in and out of the water sprinkler, she'd run toward them, forgetting her father existed.

"Do you think she's suspicious of us?" Mel asked.

"Kaylee? Absolutely not. She's too young."

"Very funny. I was referring to Frankie."

"Ah. Well, possibly. We haven't been keeping very low profiles lately."

Us. We. He liked them using those terms when describing each other.

"No, we haven't," she agreed.

"When they find out we're having a baby, they'll know why we've been talking."

Frowning, she went back to cleaning her medical equipment in the bucket of water, sponging the implements with soapy water and rinsing them in a second bucket of clean water.

Aaron could have kicked himself for being an idiot. "Let me rephrase. We are having a baby, it's true, but that's not all there is between us."

"I'm equally guilty of sending mixed signals. Because I'm confused about how I feel." She stopped scrubbing. "You confuse me, Aaron."

"I understand. That kiss the other night..." He chuckled. "It surprised me, too."

"You think it was a mistake?"

"Oh, hell no!"

"But it does make things a little messy." She resumed scrubbing.

Is that what she thought? Aaron didn't dispute her. But messy or not, he'd kiss her again in a heartbeat.

"The thing with my family—" she dried her hands "—they can go a little overboard. Interfering and calling it helping. Except for Dolores," Mel amended. "She manages to help without interfering. They should take lessons from her."

Aaron thought of his sister and parents, how they were five hundred miles away and he only got to see them once or twice a year. He'd love some interference disguised as helping.

"You're lucky to have your family close by. We can all use help now and then. I'm here today because Frankie's daughters are a lot more fun than I am, according to my daughter."

"She loves you."

"And I love her. Doesn't make me everything she needs. Children benefit from having friends their own age." He groaned and clasped his forehead. "I believe I just quoted my mother-in-law. You have my permission to throw me out on my backside."

Mel finished putting away her equipment. Aaron had the feeling she expected, or hoped, he'd say something else. What, he wasn't sure.

Samantha spared him from the continuing silence by returning from taking her horse to his stall in the minibarn.

"See you tomorrow morning," she called to Mel before joining Frankie and the girls. A moment later, she waved and headed into the house.

"What's going on tomorrow morning?" Aaron asked.

Mel shut and locked her case. "She's going with me on a couple of calls."

"Wow." Aaron gasped and grabbed a fistful of his shirtfront, pretending to have a heart attack. "Call 9-1-1."

"Very funny."

"You can't deny it's unexpected."

"Tell me about it." She gave a small laugh. "I barely recognize myself anymore."

"You're dealing with everything pretty well, if you ask me."

"Or, I'm hiding my head in the sand and praying my troubles will disappear. I'm not sure which."

Joking aside, she was saying more than she realized. Beneath her brave front, she was worried and scared and uncertain. Like him. He wanted to, *needed* to, do something to let her know he cared and that their connection was deepening. Something more than carrying heavy buckets.

He moved closer.

"Frankie's looking," Mel warned.

"Have dinner with me tonight."

"What?"

"Doesn't have to be fancy. But I want to take you out, Mel."

"Have you lost your mind?"

"We have to start making plans sometime," he said. "Why not over dinner?"

"Are we making plans or going on a date?"

"Both. Couples combine the two all the time."

She narrowed her gaze at him.

"Come on," he pressed.

"Maybe."

"Otherwise, we'll have to wait until Sunday." And it would be harder for him to get away. He tried to spend free weekends with Kaylee, and Nancy would question any change in those plans.

This, however, was important and worth risking any repercussions from Nancy.

"Where?" Mel asked.

"Wherever you want. Rio Verde. Scottsdale. Fountain Hills."

She took a long moment to respond. "Vito's Old Country."

The Italian family eatery in Rio Verde. He'd taken Kaylee there once, and she'd made a terrible mess with her spaghetti. Aaron had tipped the server extra and apologized on the way out. Would they recognize him and remember?

"Sounds good. What time?"

"Not too late." Mel checked her phone. "I have an early-morning appointment. A goat with an ear infection."

"Six thirty okay? I'd like to give Kaylee another hour at least to play with her friends."

He'd also have plenty of time to shower and change and sit with Kaylee while she ate supper.

"I'll meet you there," Mel said.

"No way. This is a date, remember? I'll pick you up."

She relented with a nod and a huff he thought might have just been for show. "I'd better hurry. Who knows what's clean in my closet."

A dress, please, Aaron thought. As much as he liked her in jeans—her curvy figure did them justice—he really wanted her to wear the dress he'd seen her in last month at the community potluck. The tiny straps and low-cut back had shown off lots of lovely bare skin.

"Daddy!" Kaylee squealed. "I want my towel."

It was right where she'd left it, folded on the lawn chair. But Kaylee was notorious for having short-term memory loss.

"Hang on a sec, kiddo."

When he swung back around, Mel was already carrying a load toward the driveway where her truck was parked. If Aaron went after her, there'd be no hiding their relationship from

Frankie. From the entire Hartman clan, really, because Mel's sister would report what she'd seen at the first available opportunity.

Then again, Aaron and Mel weren't doing anything wrong.

He hesitated for a good ten seconds before grabbing her medical case and sprinting after her. Even at a distance, he could sense the heat of Frankie's stare boring a hole in his back. Too late now.

MEL SAT BESIDE Aaron in his family SUV as they traveled the road to Rio Verde and Vito's Old Country. A dozen concerns flitted through her head, circling like hawks and making it hard for her to concentrate.

This was a bad idea. What if they ran into someone they knew at the restaurant? Thank goodness Ronnie was still practicing with Samantha when Aaron had arrived at the house to pick up Mel. This wasn't a date, she told herself, merely a strategy meeting.

Uh-huh. As if she'd wear a yellow dress and

three-inch heels to a meeting. And speaking of heels, this pair was killing her. She could already feel the sharp pinch in her toes and heels.

That was what she got for always wearing boots or going barefoot. Maybe she'd kick her shoes off under the table once they were seated.

"Sorry." She turned to Aaron. "What did you say?"

He lowered the volume on the radio, as if that was the problem. "I hear the stuffed eggplant is really good."

"I figured you for a beef man."

"I'll have you know, I'm a person of varied tastes."

He would have to grin and trigger that stupid chain reaction inside her, starting with the catch in her throat and ending with the tingle that reached all the way to her toes. He would also have to wear a turquoise cowboy shirt that matched his vivid blue eyes. Perhaps if she looked out the window…

"What's your favorite Italian dish?" he asked,

sounding an awful lot like they really were on a date.

She abandoned the window to face him. It wasn't as if she hadn't seen the local landscape a few hundred, make that a thousand, times.

"Linguini. With cream sauce. And caprese salad. But I like to try new dishes, too."

"You drink wine? When you're not pregnant, that is."

"On occasion. Chianti with Italian."

What did they usually talk about when they were together? Clearly not favorite foods or dining out. She tried to think. They'd discussed their personal situations, specifically why they couldn't date. A little bit about their pasts. Growing up in Mustang Valley and Queen Creek respectively.

Nothing meaningful, not that one's wine of choice was particularly meaningful. But there was something nice about casual conversation. Just like a regular couple.

At the restaurant, Aaron parked. Mel reached for her door handle, intending to open it.

"Hold on. I'll get that."

"You don't have to."

"I want to."

Pleased by this show of gallantry, she sat until he came around the SUV to her side and opened the door. Men in these parts tended to treat her like one of them. Especially when she was trudging through cow manure.

"Thanks." She accepted the hand he extended.

At the hostess station, she learned he'd called ahead and made a reservation. For a booth. There was a candle in the center of the table and dim lighting.

Not special. She noticed all the tables had candles. Yet, Mel felt special all the same, proving she was a secret romantic.

"I thought this was a family restaurant."

Aaron remained standing until she'd slid into the booth. "It is."

She surveyed the large room, observing mostly couples but also several parents with their children, and decided her imagination was working overtime.

Soon enough, the server left them alone, their drink and appetizer order in hand. Iced tea for Aaron, plain water for Mel and a caprese salad to share.

"What made you decide to become a vet?" he asked after their drinks arrived.

"No big secret there. I grew up in a ranching community."

"That's not an answer."

She sat back against the vinyl seat. "We had a bunch of barn cats when I was a kid. A house cat, too, but also all these half-feral ones. A mama birthed a litter of kittens in the hay trough and then a week later disappeared. I was about ten or eleven. Not long after my mom died. Dad was going to humanely euthanize the kittens. What other choice did he have? I carried on until he let me bottle raise the litter. It was a lot of work. Like 24/7 work. Luckily, it was during summer when I didn't have school."

"Did the kittens survive?"

"Yes. To everyone's surprise, including mine." She laughed softly, then sobered. "I loved it. I'd been utterly miserable and missing my mom. Suddenly, I was less miserable. Of course, Dad made me find homes for the entire litter and a few of the barn cats."

"Unexpected deaths. They're rough." Aaron covered her hand with his. Despite their size and strength, his touch was gentle and caring.

Two decades had passed, but Mel remembered every detail from those months following her mother's death. "She went riding alone all the time. She was an expert horsewoman. For whatever reason, on that ride, the horse spooked or slipped, and she fell. Hit her head on the only rock within eight feet in any direction. When the horse came galloping home without my mom, Dad figured she wasn't far behind. Two hours later, he went out looking for her. Four hours later, he reported her missing, and the authorities sent out a search party." Mel lowered her voice. "They found her the next morning. The medical examiner's report said she'd died instantly."

"I'm sure you heard this before," Aaron

squeezed her fingers, "but at least she didn't suffer."

"I'm sorry that Robin did. Truly. It must have been horrible for you. But at least you got to say goodbye to her. My mom's last words to me were, 'clean your room or we aren't going out for pizza tonight.'"

"Robin's last words were, 'it's on the bathroom shelf.'"

"What was?"

He shrugged. "I don't know. She was on high doses of pain meds, fighting a massive brain tumor and in and out of consciousness. That didn't stop me from tearing the bathroom apart after she died, searching for some secret item she left behind for me."

"That's a sad story." Mel's heart ached for him.

He released her hand when the server arrived with their salad and didn't attempt to take it again. Mel picked up her fork. Aaron, too.

"She constantly worried I'd be killed in the line of duty. Neither of us figured on her dying first. We thought we'd be together until we were old and feeble and living in a nursing home."

He spoke with such tenderness and love, Mel couldn't help being affected. They must have been incredibly happy together. Had the kind of relationship her dad did with Dolores. The kind she dreamed of but didn't think possible.

"What made you choose law enforcement?"

The agony he clearly still felt over Robin's death receded a little. "No cute story, I'm afraid. When I started college, I majored in marketing."

"A salesman! You?"

"My dad's in the business. I took a class on introduction to criminal justice just for fun and because I needed some extra credits. Next thing I knew, I'd changed over to the Police Academy Preparation Program."

Mel didn't ask what had brought him to Mustang Valley. She already knew he'd wanted a less dangerous job for Kaylee's sake.

"Did you ever have any close calls when you

worked for the Phoenix Police Department?" The salad was delicious. Mel, however, only picked at it.

"A few."

"Been shot at?"

"Yeah." He paused as if to reflect. "My partner took a bullet my first year on the force. A flesh wound. He was back on the job a month later. Six months after that, his wife divorced him. Said she couldn't take the stress."

"Robin must've been a very strong person."

"I'm convinced another reason she fought so hard to have Kaylee was she didn't want both of us to die. If I was left with a child to raise, she thought—hoped, I'm sure—I might take a less dangerous position or quit law enforcement altogether." He glanced up as their entrées arrived. "Mustang Valley's just the right speed for me. Quiet. Close-knit. Low crime rate."

Normally, Mel would savor her first bite of linguini. Their somber discussion had taken away the enjoyment of their beautifully prepared food.

Then again, there was something uplifting in sharing how they'd both learned to cope with loss.

"Speaking of crime," she said, "any new developments with the horse rustling?"

"Nothing so far. I'm going to the barrel-racing event this coming weekend at the Silver Spur Arena."

"Really? Why?"

"Wherever horse people gather, there's bound to be talk. I thought I might learn something of interest. And it'll be fun for Kaylee."

"We're going, too. Samantha's competing."

"I heard." His voice took on an intimate quality.

Was her being at the event part of his reason for going?

"Not sure how much information I'll get," he said, "but I have to try. The thieves are from this area, I'm sure of it, or at least in partnership with someone who is."

"Someone like whom?"

Aaron stabbed at his stuffed eggplant. "This

person, if there is one, would have pretty intimate knowledge of the horse setups around the valley."

She laughed. "You're describing me."

"Maybe I should check you out. Thoroughly." His eyes darkened and dipped to her neck, igniting that stupid chain reaction again.

"Maybe you should."

Was she actually flirting? This was crazy. They hadn't even flirted when they first met.

She recalled Aaron speaking about his late wife and the expression on his face when he did. Her mood immediately sank.

Flirting was one thing. Love, another. He'd had that once with Robin, his obvious soul mate. Mel couldn't expect anything remotely close to that, and wishing for it would only bring her pain.

What would it be like to be loved by Aaron? Robin's life had been cut short, but she'd been one incredibly lucky woman to have been the object of Aaron's adoration.

Mel set down her fork. Who was she fooling?

No way could she compete with Robin's memory. The best possible circumstances were she and Aaron getting along, him being a great date and them united in giving their child a wonderful upbringing.

"I'm going to take care of you and the baby, Mel."

Shoot. He must have guessed her thoughts. She wasn't always guarded with her emotions.

"You don't have to take care of me, Aaron. I'm quite capable of supporting myself and the baby."

He shook his head. "You're not really going to pull the old independent woman act?"

"Yes," she conceded. "I'll accept your help and support. We can share custody. Swap weeks when the baby's a little older."

"Is that what you want?"

His sincerity momentarily threw her, prompting her to answer in kind. "Honestly, I always figured I'd be married when I started a family."

And in love, she silently added. *The way you were in love with Robin.*

"We can talk about that. Down the road."

Memories of her father saying he'd offered to marry Carrie Anne flashed in her head. He might have done the right thing according to some, but Mel wanted more than a husband who proposed simply out of duty and not love.

"No rush. Lots of couples raise their child together without being married."

After that, Mel and Aaron never quite regained the fun, flirty camaraderie from earlier. For the rest of the meal, they discussed Kaylee, Mel's nieces, Mel's progress with Samantha's horse and how the orphan foal wasn't doing as well as Mel would have liked.

In the parking lot, Aaron took her arm, just as she'd expected. That didn't stop her from enjoying the feel of his strong fingers on her skin, the heady scent of his aftershave and the occasional bump and brush of his body against hers. She was reminded of the many times she'd lain beside him, her leg draped over his and her fingertips drawing patterns on his bare chest.

At his SUV, he opened the passenger door, re-

218   *A Baby for the Deputy*

peating his chivalry from earlier. She was about to climb in when he caught her by the wrist and tugged her into his embrace.

Ignoring the other patrons returning to their vehicles, she met Aaron's stare, searching his eyes for the look she'd seen when he talked about Robin. It wasn't there. The hunger burning in them, however, did give her a sensual thrill, and she involuntarily arched into him.

All right, not involuntarily. She very much wanted his arms circling her waist and drawing her close. She also wanted him to kiss her. Wildly and without restraint, like the other night.

When he threaded his fingers into her hair, she leaned her head back. When he nuzzled her ear, she sighed. When his lips skimmed the column of her neck, she moaned softly. When he whispered her name, she melted.

Finally, thankfully, his mouth found hers and took it possessively. Pressing her against the SUV, he trapped her between the rear door and the long length of him. As his tongue swept into her mouth, she relished in the familiar, exciting taste of him.

Aaron certainly knew how to kiss. Hard and demanding. Gentle and coaxing. She took what he offered and gave in return. Of their own volition, her hands worked their way up his back to his shoulders. There, they gripped the hard muscles and brought him closer—if that was possible. When he would have broken off the kiss, Mel refused to release him. Not until she was fully satisfied.

By the time they were in his SUV and driving toward her house, Mel was almost sorry they weren't going to the motel instead. It wasn't very far.

Chapter Nine

Aaron wasn't disappointed he and Mel had skipped the motel tonight. Okay, that wasn't entirely accurate. But he hadn't wanted her thinking sex was the only thing between them. Besides, he'd enjoyed their interplay during dinner, and the kiss in the parking lot afterward had tested the limits of his willpower.

Whatever was changing between them, and he still wasn't able to define it, had affected every aspect of their relationship, including intimacy.

Could be he was more disappointed about not

going to the motel than he first thought. She'd looked so pretty tonight, her hair loose around her shoulders rather than twisted into her usual braid. Her skin aglow in the candlelight. Her mouth full and wide and impossible not to kiss.

Pregnancy certainly agreed with her. Then again, it might be those changing feelings affecting how he perceived her.

Pulling into the garage, Aaron jangled his keys as he walked into the house, his steps light, his mood elevated.

Kaylee was awake, something immediately apparent when he entered the kitchen.

"Hey, kiddo. Why aren't you in bed?" She should have been asleep an hour ago.

"I had a bad dream." She sat at the table, a glass of milk and half an English muffin in front of her.

"That's not good." He sat beside her and tweaked her nose.

Her silly giggle washed over him, elevating his mood even higher.

There was probably no bad dream. Kaylee

used that as an excuse whenever she had trouble falling asleep or woke up after a short time. The excuse worked better on her grandmother than Aaron, landing her a little extra attention.

Speaking of which...

"Where's Gramma?" Aaron stole a sip of her milk.

"On the phone."

"Really?" She didn't usually leave Kaylee alone for any length of time. And it was late for a phone call.

"Tell me a story about Mama?" Kaylee pleaded when she was done eating.

"You got it."

He scooped her into his arms and carried her down the hall to her bedroom, passing Nancy's room as he did. The older woman sat on her bed, her phone glued to her ear. Seeing him, alarm flashed across her face. He tilted his head at Kaylee's room, indicating he was putting her to bed.

"Gramma must have an important call," he

said, drawing the sheet up to Kaylee's neck and dropping down beside her.

She snuggled with a well-worn and well-loved stuffed bear, and he began telling one of her favorite stories about how Robin broke the news to him that she was pregnant.

"When I got home from work, there was a big teddy bear sitting on the counter with a pink pacifier tied to the bow around its neck." He poked the stuffed bear's stomach.

"Why pink?"

"Because she wanted a little girl."

"Were you surprised?" Kaylee gazed up at him, her expression so reminiscent of Robin's.

"Very surprised."

The story took five more minutes to finish. Kaylee wouldn't allow Aaron to skip a single part, despite having memorized every word. When he was done, he stood and kissed her on the forehead.

"Go to sleep now. I love you."

"Love you too, Daddy." She curled her fingers into the shape of a heart and held them to her chest.

He left the door partially open behind him and headed toward the kitchen, planning to shut off the lights before going to bed himself. Shonda was expecting him tomorrow morning at the crack of dawn.

He found Nancy sitting at the table, nursing a cup of tea and wearing a scowl. Strange, she usually retired early herself.

"You're still up," he said.

"We need to talk." Her clipped tone put him on the defensive.

"What's wrong?"

"Sit down."

Aaron tolerated a lot from Nancy, including her often short temper and surliness, because she adored Kaylee, was a wonderful grandmother and helped him enormously with daycare. He also understood he was the closest target when it came to venting her heartache over the loss of her only child.

Not that she blamed him or held him responsible for Robin's brain tumor. If anything, Aaron had fought hard to extend Robin's life. Nancy's grief was simply overwhelming and beyond her abilities to cope with most days.

But she was making progress, if slow. No one had celebrated more than Aaron when she joined the Bunko group. If she wouldn't attend counseling or support groups, at least she was getting out once in a while and making friends.

"That was Winnie Hensley on the phone." She paused, apparently waiting for him to make a connection. "From church."

"Okay."

"She and her husband were at Vito's Old Country tonight, having dinner."

Aaron said nothing as the pieces fell into place.

"She saw you," Nancy accused.

He refused to volunteer any information. There was a big difference between seeing him and Mel sitting together in a booth and them kissing in the parking lot.

"Why didn't she say hi?" he asked, feigning mild interest.

"You were occupied. Having dinner with Melody Hartman."

"I see." Tiring, he cut to the chase. "Before I get upset, why don't you just say what's on your mind?"

"You were on a date with another woman."

"I was on a date with *a* woman. Not *another*."

Nancy became flustered. "H-how could you?"

He was glad her friend Winnie missed seeing Aaron and Mel's scorching kiss and that Nancy hadn't learned about their evenings at the motel. "Mel and I are friends."

"Winnie said you looked pretty cozy."

He considered insisting the dinner was strictly business. Mel *was* helping him with the horse thefts. Instead, he came clean.

There was a reason he'd been careless lately about hiding his relationship with Mel. The fact was, he'd grown weary of sneaking around and suspected Mel had, too. He subconsciously, and possibly consciously, felt ready to go public, even before Mel got pregnant.

Time to start preparing Nancy. "We were on a date," he admitted.

"Oh, no." Her face crumpled, and she swallowed a sob. "I don't believe it."

Out of respect for her distress, he gentled his tone. "It's been three years, Nancy. Even Robin would expect me to start dating again."

"But Melody Hartman?" Nancy made a face.

He was slightly offended. No, a lot offended. "Mel's a great gal."

"She may be great, but she's isn't very...ladylike."

What worse insult had Nancy been about to utter? And if she'd seen Mel in that sundress and sexy sandals, the last thing she'd be calling her was unladylike.

Comparisons were bound to happen, and Nancy was comparing Mel to Robin. He decided not to get upset about it and try a different approach instead.

"You like Dolores. And you're always saying

how nice Frankie is when we go to the café. I'm sure you'd like Mel, too, if you got to know her."

Nancy's eyes widened in alarm. "Is there a reason I need to? How serious is this?"

Aaron changed his mind. This wasn't the right moment to tell her about the baby. "I will always love Robin and miss her. She's the mother of my child, and that won't ever change. But chances are, I'll eventually meet someone new and possibly marry again. You need to accept that."

"She sacrificed months of her life for Kaylee. And you promised her to always put Kaylee first. Above everything and anyone else."

"I do put Kaylee first."

"What about when you work late?"

"My job provides a decent roof over her head, food on the table and a roomful of toys. I call that making her a priority."

"Instead of being home with her, you went on a date."

Aaron had spent almost the entire day with

Kaylee. Even so, the invisible dagger Nancy thrust hit its mark.

He had made a commitment to cherish and honor Robin's memory. Promised to put Kaylee first. Told Nancy she was a welcomed and valued member of his family for as long as she wanted.

On the other hand, Mel was pregnant, and he had an obligation to her, too, as well as their baby.

When had things become so complicated? Why had he let them? What had he been thinking, sleeping with Mel when he wasn't willing to do right by her? Aaron didn't have a high opinion of himself at the moment.

Remembering how she'd looked at dinner and the sparks that had flared between them when they'd kissed was part of the answer. She was hard to resist. But, perhaps he should. For the time being, anyway. At least until Nancy became more accustomed to the idea.

He got up from the table.

"Where are you going?" she demanded. "We're not done talking."

"I have to be up at five."

"What about Melody Hartman?"

He pushed in his chair. "I'm going to keep seeing her."

"Have you considered Kaylee? She may not accept a woman in her life who isn't her mother."

"She's young. Mel's nieces are her friends." Aaron stopped at the doorway, thinking Kaylee would like Mel and just might love having a baby brother or sister.

"She'll forget about Robin."

That, Aaron suspected, was the real reason for Nancy's objections.

"I won't let her," he said with utmost sincerity. "And neither will you."

EYES CLEAR AND BRIGHT. Ears pricked forward. Attentive and alert. No fever. No lameness. No swelling or tenderness. The horse, a sleek and muscular roan with proved speed and agility, was the epitome of health.

"He's ready to rock and roll," Mel said, finishing her routine exam.

Samantha's worried expression eased a tiny fraction. After Big John's injury, she'd probably always fret before a competition. And this particular horse belonged to Ronnie, not Samantha. A lot of responsibility and yet another reason for her to be chewing her nails to the quick.

"You'll do great," Mel assured her. "You were flying at practice last night."

She'd had a vet call near Powell Ranch and decided to drop by and observe the practice. That was the excuse she told herself, anyway, not admitting to a much-needed distraction from her many problems.

Despite her pregnancy being confirmed for almost two weeks now, she'd yet to do anything about it other than visit her doctor, purchase prenatal vitamins, struggle with bras that were becoming tight and painful, and discover plain crackers and ginger ale helped with the morning sickness.

Sure, she and Aaron talked daily, and he'd been adamant about providing for the baby. But no specifics had been decided, and she wasn't telling her family until at least a basic plan was in place.

"I'm still getting used to him." Samantha absently groomed the horse, running a thick brush over his flank. "He thinks and reacts differently than Big John."

She'd gone twice with Mel this week on calls, and Mel had heard the entire lowdown on the horse to the smallest detail.

Ronnie appeared from behind the trailer, stared long and hard at Samantha and said, "Shouldn't you have saddled up by now?"

"Yeah. Mel was just examining the horse."

"It's hot. You'd better take him to the water trough for a drink."

"I will. Give me a minute, okay?"

It wasn't *what* they said as much as the *way* they spoke to each other that had Mel paying close attention. The friction was undeniable and uncomfortable and apparently brand-new.

Had something happened between yesterday and today that set them off? A difference of opinion, perhaps? Could be stress, Mel supposed. Ronnie's temper always flared before a competition, though she wasn't the one climbing into the saddle today.

Later, perhaps, when she and Ronnie were alone, she'd ask what was going on. Then, Ronnie would probably ask her the same question and bring up Aaron. Not what she needed at the moment.

Returning from stowing her medical case in her truck, she grabbed the bridle hanging from a hook on the side of the trailer and handed it to Samantha. The young woman had finished saddling the horse, triple checking the cinch and adjusting the length of the stirrups. Only the bridle remained. And herself.

She'd yet to fix her hair and change into nice boots and her fancy show chaps. The competition wasn't an official rodeo event, but that

didn't change the fact competitors were expected to adhere to a certain dress code. Horses,
too. This roan's coat shone, and he wore tack
decorated with gleaming silver conchos.

"You're going to get dirty," Mel said when
the horse bumped his nose against Samantha's
clean dress shirt sleeve. "Let me."

She bridled the horse while Samantha braided
her hair, tied it with a ribbon and applied
makeup, using the truck's side mirror to view
her handiwork. Mel was struck with a sudden
sentimental pang. How many times had she
seen Ronnie do the same thing before an event?

Glancing about, she searched for her errant
sister. Apparently, she'd left to help another stu-
dent prepare.

The person she did spot was Aaron, carrying
his young daughter and accompanied by his
mother-in-law. They made a charming picture,
Dad, daughter and grandmother.

Mel's hands suddenly went still and only the
horse bobbing his head prompted her to finish
her task. She automatically buckled the bridle

and straightened the reins, her mind wandering and wondering where she and her child would fit into that picture.

At the entrance to the bleachers, Aaron parted from Kaylee and her grandmother. He then went off to join a group of local ranchers gathered at the arena fence. What was it he'd said? Whenever horse folk gathered, they talked, and worthwhile leads could come from the most unexpected sources.

"Thanks," Samantha said, appearing beside Mel.

"Sure." Mel realized she'd just been standing there, staring. Patting the horse's neck was a poor cover-up, but she did it anyway. "No problem."

"This is the first time I've ever competed when my parents weren't here to watch me." Samantha's voice broke.

"I'm sure they'd like to be here." *And would be if they knew about it.*

Without asking, Mel took the paper entrant number and motioned for Samantha to turn

236 A Baby for the Deputy

around. She pinned the square, with the Mustang Valley Feed and Supply Depot name and logo printed in bold letters, to Samantha's back, thinking again how often she'd done the same for Ronnie.

When she finished, Samantha suddenly threw herself at Mel, practically knocking her off balance. While not ready to call her "sister," Mel returned the hug with genuine emotion. Without her parents there, Samantha was obviously in need of a friend.

"I'll be rooting for you from the stands," Mel said, extracting herself.

"Can I go to work with you on Monday?"

"We'll see."

"Frankie's off that day. She won't need me to babysit."

Not for the first time, Mel considered Samantha helping her more as her pregnancy advanced. She'd wait and see, however. Samantha might patch things up with her parents and leave Mustang Valley.

"I'll see you after the event." She patted Samantha's shoulder. "Good luck."

Samantha's group was the last to go and included those individuals competing on a professional level. The first group, comprised ages twelve and under, was always popular with the crowd. The youngsters might be small in size and less experienced, but they were incredibly daring and talented.

Stopping at the refreshment stand for a cold soda, Mel wandered toward the bleachers. She'd spotted her dad and Dolores earlier and went in search of them again.

Zigzagging through the crowd, she almost ran smack into Aaron. He'd left the group of ranchers and retrieved Kaylee from her grandmother. The pair stood before her, Aaron as startled to see Mel as she was to see him.

"Hi." She fumbled with her hands. "You're here."

He simply grinned.

"What's so funny?"

"I'm just happy to see you."

Was he? Then why hadn't he asked her out again? He'd had plenty of opportunities.

"How's the investigation coming?"

"Nothing good yet." He shifted Kaylee to his other side. The little girl wore a neon pink cap and purple shorts and looked absolutely adorable. "But the evening's young."

A truck with the feed store logo on the side drove past them, its loud engine momentarily preventing conversation. Neighboring businesses were often recruited to sponsor community events, and the feed store could always be counted on to pay for an advertising banner as well as participant numbers.

Once the truck had passed, Mel said, "Well, um, take care," certain she sounded awkward and confused.

"Do you mind?" Aaron abruptly thrust Kaylee at her. "Guillermo's here, and I'd like to talk to him."

Mel gasped, automatically holding out her arms to accept the little girl. "Wait!"

Too late. Aaron was gone, jogging off toward

the man Mel recognized as a grain rep who worked the area. She understood Aaron's haste. The man got around and sold to most of the ranches in Mustang Valley. He also had a tendency to swear a blue streak. Not the sort of language appropriate for a three-year-old, and Aaron probably hadn't wanted Kaylee to hear that.

Of course, she started to cry.

"Hey, there," Mel said, bouncing Kaylee. "You remember me? I'm Paige and Sienna's aunt."

That earned her a wary stare. Okay, Kaylee wasn't a baby. Maybe Mel was better off entertaining her rather than rocking her. It wasn't as if she lacked experience with preschoolers.

Which reminded her, where were Frankie and Mel's nieces? Just when Mel needed them most, as a playmate for Kaylee, they were MIA.

"Come on," she said. "Let's go look at some of the pretty horses."

She set Kaylee down, and together they walked over to the arena fence. Mel wanted to stick close by should Aaron come looking for them. Some of the competitors were warming up in the arena, walking, trotting or slow loping their horses to loosen muscles and acclimate them to the commotion.

"See the white horse over there?" Mel received another stare from Kaylee and sighed. "I don't blame you." She took Kaylee's hand. "I would be unhappy if my dad left me with a stranger."

Not that Mel was exactly a stranger. She was intimately acquainted with Kaylee's father and carrying the girl's baby brother or sister.

What a sobering thought. Mel glanced down, studying the girl. Under different circumstances, she might have been Kaylee's stepmom. They were certainly going to be better acquainted in the future. However Mel and Aaron worked out the custody agreement, their child would eventually be spending time at his house with him and Kaylee.

Also with Nancy, Kaylee's grandmother. An even more sobering thought.

"I like the tan horse with the white stockings. See?" Mel pointed.

Kaylee actually looked.

"He reminds me of the baby horse I'm taking care of. He's really cute. Like you."

At last, Kaylee responded with a tentative smile.

"Maybe your dad will bring you out to see the baby horse. I could ask him."

The little girl nodded.

Success! Mel felt a rush of pleasure. She wanted to be on good terms with Aaron's daughter.

For whatever reason, the thought brought a lump to her throat. She blamed pregnancy hormones. It also might have to do with Kaylee and Mel being kindred spirits—they both had or would have a surprise half sibling. Both their families had suffered a great loss with the death of a loved one. And, for the moment, they'd both been abandoned by Aaron.

All right, abandoned was too strong a word. Aaron was returning for Kaylee any minute.

And he hadn't exactly abandoned Mel, either. Rather, he'd been taking some necessary alone time this past week to sort things out. At least, she wanted to believe that was his reason for not suggesting a second date.

Drat. Tears? Really? She wiped angrily at her eyes.

"Are you sad?" Kaylee asked.

"No, no." She patted the girl's head, oddly soothed by the soft texture of her silky curls. "I'm fine."

"What are you doing with her!"

At the brusque question, Mel and Kaylee both turned. Nancy stood there, holding two drinks and a box of popcorn.

"Gramma!" Kaylee hurried to Nancy, arms outstretched. "I'm thirsty."

"Where's Aaron?" Bristling, Nancy handed Kaylee a juice box.

"He's over there talking to the grain rep." Mel refused to be intimidated. "He asked me to watch Kaylee."

"Why didn't he wait for me?"

"He was in a hurry."

Kaylee didn't appear to notice the tension or didn't care. She was busy emptying her juice box as fast as possible.

"Gramma, look at the horse." The one with the white stockings happened to be trotting by them, delighting Kaylee. "I want to go riding."

"You can't today, darling."

Everything about Nancy changed when she addressed her granddaughter. Her voice, her expression, her manner, all softened around the edges. Mel was almost convinced that between her obvious love for Kaylee and Dolores being her friend, Nancy had a nice side. But, as the saying goes, she spoke too soon.

"I need to talk to you." Nancy's glance, tender a moment ago, cooled. "As long as you're here. And if you don't mind."

Mel breathed deeply to calm he nerves. She'd never been alone with Nancy before. They'd conversed only once, briefly at her dad's birthday party when Dolores introduced them and before Samantha's big scene.

"Um, sure. About anything in particular?" Mel shifted, praying Nancy had a sick pet and wanted free medical advice. She knew better, however. This had to do with Aaron.

"I've enjoyed playing Bunko with your step-mother and her friends."

They moved toward the fence, following Kaylee who wanted a closer look at the horses.

"Dolores's group is a great bunch of ladies."

"They are. They've made me feel welcome." Nancy rested a fond hand on the top of Kaylee's head.

Mel had been doing the same thing a few minutes ago. Didn't mean she felt a connection to the other woman. If anything, the opposite was true. Mel wasn't sure she'd ever be able to warm up to Nancy. She would try, though. For Aaron's sake and their baby's.

"I admit," Nancy continued, "it was hard when we first moved here."

"I can imagine."

"Robin had passed just six months earlier."

"I'm very sorry for your loss." Mel wasn't

sure what else to say or where this conversation was going. Nancy didn't keep her waiting.

"She and Aaron were so much in love. And I'm not simply saying that because Robin...because they didn't get to spend their entire lives together. They were happy. Ecstatic, really. A bright, beautiful future ahead of them." She paused. "No one expected Robin to get sick."

Mel did sympathize. "It was like that when my mom died. One day, she was there. The next day, she wasn't."

Nancy considered Mel's remark, her hand still resting on Kaylee's head. "Yes. Very tragic. You would understand. Loving someone so very much, then losing them. Each of us handles grief differently, and we don't always act in our best interests or that of others."

Mel immediately thought of her father and his involvement with Carrie Anne.

"Aaron's duty lies with Kaylee," Nancy said. "She's the most important person in his life. He will never let Robin down or dishonor her memory by doing something he'd regret. It's what I respect and admire the most about him. What everyone does." She narrowed her gaze at Mel. "As I'm sure you do, too."

Nancy clearly knew, or at least suspected, that Mel and Aaron were involved. And she was issuing a not-so-subtle warning for Mel to stay away.

She should be annoyed, possibly offended, only she wasn't.

Nothing like having someone hold up a mirror to your face. Mel could suddenly see herself through Nancy's eyes and didn't like the person staring back at her. Reasonably, rationally, she could argue that Aaron was free to date. That wouldn't alleviate Nancy's pain or make what Mel and Aaron were doing right.

"My family's waiting for me," she said, excusing herself. "Bye, Kaylee." She waved. "See you soon."

Nancy wore a satisfied smile. "Nice talking to you."

A minute later, and out of Nancy's eyesight, Mel stopped, her heart racing. With trembling fingers, she pulled out her cell phone and texted Aaron, letting him know Kaylee was with her grandmother.

After he responded, she texted back that she wanted to get together later that week when they were both free. She didn't add they simply could not continue in this limbo state any longer. She'd save that discussion for when they met.

Chapter Ten

The crowd broke into applause as the rider finished her run, crossing in front of the electronic timer at a full gallop. The young woman, close to Samantha in age, slowed her horse to a trot, then to a walk. Circling to the left, she listened for her results to be announced. The spectators quieted, also listening.

"Sixteen-point-five."

Frowning, the young woman turned her horse toward the exit gate and rode through.

"She cut that last barrel too wide," Frankie

said. "Lost a good half a second on her time. She's in fourth place."

Half a second? Mel shook her head. Hard to believe the first four places were separated by tenths of a second. That was true, however, with a lot of sports. One had only to watch the Olympics.

"We aren't even halfway through the class." Mel fanned herself with the paper number an earlier competitor from the junior class had left behind and wished she'd worn a hat with a wider brim.

Samantha was one of the last competitors to go, which could be to her advantage. She'd have the opportunity to study the other riders and possibly modify her strategy.

"Dad and Dolores still down there?" Mel switched the paper number to her other hand, using it as a shield against the blinding glare of the setting sun. Last she'd seen her parents, they were with Samantha and Ronnie, offering help and moral support and most likely getting in the way.

"Grandpa said he would buy us ice cream." Paige bounced up and down in the bleachers, enjoying the noise it made. Other nearby people, not so much.

"He will." Frankie rested a hand on her daughter's knee, silently encouraging her to stop.

"I'm bored," Sienna complained, also getting a pat from her mother.

The twin girls sat, one on each side of Frankie, with Mel beside Sienna. They were growing increasingly restless and tired of hearing their mother say, "Be good." They wanted to play with their friend Kaylee, but the little girl's grandmother had vetoed that idea with an "It's not safe," even though Frankie had volunteered to supervise. Mel supposed she was the real reason behind Nancy's refusal.

She caught a glimpse of grandmother and granddaughter from the corner of her eye, then risked a longer look. They were seated a few rows down and over from Mel, close enough for Kaylee to see her young friends, but too far to interact. During one of those times Kaylee had snuck a peek, Mel summoned the courage to wave. She'd received a tiny wave in return, just enough to make her smile.

The next instant, Nancy had glanced backward, and Mel quickly lowered her hand. It had been a stupid idea to begin with. She might win over Kaylee eventually, but Nancy was another story.

While Frankie attempted to entertain the twins with one of the emergency toys she always stashed in her purse, Mel scanned the crowd for Aaron. He'd been busy chatting up as many people as possible. Mel knew this because she'd been keeping tabs on him. He'd apparently been keeping tabs on her, as well. More than once, their gazes had connected.

"Thanks for helping with Samantha," Frankie said. "It means a lot to her."

Mel abandoned her efforts to locate Aaron. "To be honest, I didn't do it for Samantha. I did it for you."

"Yeah, I know. She still appreciates it. As do I."

The girls were enthralled by a handheld game and not paying attention to the grown-ups.

"What changed your mind?" Frankie asked. "You never told me."

"Nothing. I simply reconsidered."

"Ha, ha, ha."

"It wasn't a joke."

"Come on," Frankie insisted. "Something's been bothering you lately."

"A half sister we had no idea existed showing up out of the blue isn't enough to bother me?"

"Since before then. You've been preoccupied for the last month or two."

If anyone would understand Mel's situation besides Dolores, it was her older sister. She'd given birth to and raised twin girls without ever telling their father and slaved at the café in order to give them a decent home. All without any help. Other than the lottery money, that was, and every cent of her share had gone into the purchase of her house.

She was the definition of independent single mother. Mel could learn a lot from her. And

Frankie would appreciate Mel's uncertainty regarding Aaron's feelings for her, having been through a similar situation with her ex-boyfriend.

"I...um..." Mel struggled. "Have some news."

"What? Tell me."

"Okay. Relax. This isn't easy." She checked on the girls, who had switched places in order to sit together and play. "I'm..." She gestured with her hand, showing a rounded belly.

Frankie's eyes nearly popped out of her head. "No kidding! You're—"

"Shh." Mel's glance cut to the girls and the couple on the other side who were clients of Ronnie's. "I've only told three people so far. Well, two. Dolores sort of figured it out."

"The father is one of those people, I hope."

"Yeah," she reluctantly admitted.

"Who is he? And when did you start dating? Is he from out of town?" She gasped. "Did you meet at that seminar?"

"No. He's, ah—"

"I can't believe you were flirting with Aaron

the other day, and you're pregnant with another man's baby."

Frankie was one of the smartest people Mel had ever met. Yet, she certainly wasn't using all of her brain cells today. Mel sighed expansively.

"I *was* flirting with the father."

"Aaron! Seriously?"

"Not so loud."

"Holy cow. This is unbelievable." Frankie took a moment to assimilate the news. "What are you going to do?" she finally asked in a half whisper.

"I only recently found out. We're still in the figuring-out phase. Plus, he hasn't told Nancy yet. Though, she suspects we've been seeing each other and isn't happy. She gave me a less than subtle stay-away warning earlier."

"Here?"

"Right before the barrel racing started."

"Ooh. Not cool." Frankie helped the girls figure out the next step to the game. "What did you do?"

"Nothing much. Let her talk. I truly understand where she's coming from. Aaron told me from the start he wasn't ready for a committed relationship, and neither am I."

"Uh, excuse me, Mel. You're having a..." She mimicked Mel's big belly gesture. "That's a commitment. A big one. He needs to step up. Financially, if anything."

Mel must have misunderstood her sister. "I'm surprised to hear you say that. You didn't tell—" She caught herself before mentioning Spence's name. "You-know-who."

"No, I didn't."

An odd note penetrated Frankie's voice. One Mel hadn't heard before.

"Do you regret not telling him?"

"Constantly." Frankie nodded at her girls. "Every time I look at them."

"Then why not call him?"

"It's complicated."

Mel snorted. "Tell me."

"You-know-who is completely untrustworthy. Nothing like Aaron. Now there's someone with a great job. A daughter he loves. Roots to the community. Responsible, reliable, a family man. Look how he puts up with Nancy."

"I hear she's not that bad. Dolores likes her, and Kaylee adores her."

"Dolores likes everyone, and Kaylee's her granddaughter. But we were talking about Aaron, not Nancy. He's a great guy. He'll be good to you and the baby. Take care of you both."

Mel noticed Frankie hadn't mentioned love. Was her sister's heart that hardened? Granted, Spence had hurt her. In Mel's opinion, that didn't justify her not telling him about the girls. But the decision was her sister's to make, not Mel's. And she was expecting the same treatment from Frankie and the rest of her family— being allowed to choose her own path without criticism or interference. She'd settle for no less.

"I can give you the name and number of my attorney if you want," Frankie said.

"Since when do you have an attorney?"

"He's mostly on standby. But he has given me some pretty good advice if you-know-who ever contacts me."

"Did he advise you to tell you-know-who about you-know-what?"

"He might have mentioned it. But, again, we're talking about you. Not me. Aaron can and should pay you child support."

"He's already offered."

"That's good."

Frankie tapped her girls' shoulders and motioned to the arena, telling them to watch. Mel noticed that Samantha had mounted her horse and was waiting by the gate for her turn.

"Duty and responsibility are very high on Aaron's list."

"I'm actually surprised he hasn't proposed," Frankie said. "He just strikes me as an old-fashioned kind of guy."

Mel pictured Aaron's expression when he talked about his late wife at dinner. How she wanted her future husband to look at her the same way.

"I wouldn't accept."

"How far along are you, anyway?"

"About seven weeks."

"A lot can change between now and the big day."

Mel supposed her sister was right. Much had changed already.

"You could do a lot worse than Aaron."

Again, Mel snorted. "You make it sound like I won third prize in a contest."

"I'm just saying, you might want to think hard about latching on to him. If you don't, some other woman will. He's too good-looking. And then there's that uniform." Frankie nudged Mel and gave her a wink. "That's what did it for you, right?"

They managed to drop the subject, for which Mel was infinitely glad, when Samantha took her run at the barrels. Her performance was practically flawless and at the speed of light. Her time put her in first place, a position she held through the remainder of the event. Mel and Frankie clapped and whooped loudly when her name was announced at the end, and she was presented with her prize.

While the entire family gathered at the horse trailer, Mel considered the similarities between her situation and Samantha's mother with a fresh eye.

Had she been unfair to her father? He wasn't so different from Aaron. Grieving the loss of a late wife and reluctant to introduce a new romantic interest to his family for fear of their negative reaction.

Watching him unsaddle the horse and issue instructions to Samantha, just like he'd done when Mel and her sisters were younger, a small dam broke inside her. The next moment, she went to him, determined to make amends. To her delight, he greeted her with an affectionate smile.

"There's my pretty Melody."

"And there's my handsome dad." She stood on tiptoes and kissed his cheek.

Chuckling, he rubbed the spot. "What's that for?"

"Just cuz."

She half expected him to mention their minor tiff. Instead, he gave her a big squeeze. "I love you, hon."

Suddenly, Mel wanted to tell him about the baby. This was big. Life changing. Her father was too important not to include him. Maybe this wasn't the best time or place, but she decided to follow her heart.

"Hey." She took his arm. "Come walk with me."

"What's up?"

"I have something to share with you. If you have a second."

"For you, always."

"You have to promise to keep this a secret," she said when they were far enough away not to be overheard. "Except for Dolores. She knows already."

"Knows what?"

Mel stopped to look her father in the face and take his hand in hers. "I'm pregnant. And I'm very happy about it, so please don't worry."

"That's like asking the sun not to shine." He

hung his head, more in confusion than disappointment. Like everyone else, he'd had no idea
she was involved with anyone. "Who's the father?"

"Promise me you won't talk to him."

"Is he going to do right by you?"

"If you mean, is he going to pay child support
and help raise our child, then yes."

"But not marry you."

"I don't want to get married, Dad. My choice."

"Then why did you…you… Dammit, Mel,
why'd you sleep with him?"

"We were careful."

"Apparently not careful enough. And you still
didn't say who he is."

"Please, Dad." She fought back a sudden surge
of emotion. "I really need your support now.
Not to make things harder on me."

He inhaled deeply. "Fine, fine. I won't shove
my fist into his face. Promise," he added when
she glowered at him.

"It's Aaron," she admitted softly.

"Aaron!"

"Shh. Not so loud." Mel glanced around, worried they'd been heard.

"And here I was just starting to like him."

"No reason you shouldn't. He's a great guy. And I think he'll be a good dad."

"Can't be all that great if he won't—"

"Dad!" Mel rolled her eyes.

"I'm looking out for you."

"And I don't want that to ever change. But you have to let me, let Aaron and me, decide what's best for us."

"Your sister Frankie didn't marry Spence."

"This is different," Mel insisted. "She never told Spence she was pregnant. Aaron knows and will be an involved father."

"I still don't like it."

"I get that." She gave his generous waist a squeeze. "I wouldn't have you any other way."

During their walk back to rejoin the family, she reminded him to keep quiet until Aaron had a chance to tell Nancy and Kaylee. Mustang Valley was a small enough community that word traveled. And while he wasn't happy

about her single state, she had no doubt what-
soever he'd be just as wonderful of a grandfather to her child as he was to her sister Frankie's
daughters.

Once the horse was finally loaded and the
equipment stowed, the family collectively
agreed to meet back at Mel's dad's house for
pizza and a dip in the pool. If the girls got tired,
they could always sleep in the spare room.

Mel strolled along with them to the parking
lot where they went their separate ways. Rounding the row of parked vehicles, she spotted her
truck—and the tall, lanky figure in boots and
jeans leaning on the hood.

"I was hoping to find you," Aaron said when
she neared, his sexy grin in full force. "Got a
minute?"

"Be strong," she murmured, only to have her
feet disobey her instructions and hurry toward
him.

AARON AND MEL wandered leisurely across the
quickly emptying parking area. On impulse,

he took her hand and when she didn't object, linked their fingers.

By now, the sun had long set. Parking-lot lights cast inky shadows that moved and shifted every few feet.

"Where's Kaylee and Nancy?" she asked.

"Driving home. We came separately in case I was called away."

"Do you do that a lot? Take separate vehicles?"

"Not really. Today was a special circumstance." He didn't mention the arrangement had worked out in his favor. Otherwise, he and Mel wouldn't be together now.

"By the way." She sent him a sidelong glance. "Where are we going?"

She'd accepted his request to accompany him without question. But apparently her trust had limits for he was sensing some hesitancy. He tried to put her at ease with a smile.

"I made, oh, let's call it, dinner plans."

"What kind of plans?" Suspicion crept into her voice.

"Come on. Take a chance." Aaron led her to his SUV, opened the rear compartment and removed a small, personal-size ice chest. Flipping open the top, he produced two cold cans of soda and two foil-wrapped sandwiches.

Letting her choose a soda—she picked orange—he handed her a sandwich.

Mel lifted a corner of the foil and raised her brows. "Peanut butter and jelly?"

"The best the snack bar had to offer."

"I see."

He wasn't deterred by her disdain. "It's late. You must be hungry. Especially since you skipped lunch."

"What makes you think that?"

"I know more about you than you realize. For instance, you get busy and forget to eat."

"I happened to have had an apple and protein bar for lunch today."

"That's all? Next time, add a big glass of milk. Starving isn't good for the baby." He perched on the SUV's rear compartment and then patted the spot beside him. "Sit. Take a load off."

She ducked her head and plunked down beside him, carefully arranging herself so only their knees touched.

"I'm supposed to be having pizza at Dad's."

"Consider this an appetizer."

"Only because you're right. I am hungry." She ripped open the foil and bit into the sandwich.

If he'd known he could bribe her with peanut butter and jelly, he'd have done it sooner.

Swallowing, she asked, "Make any progress on the horse thefts today?"

"I learned there's a new ranch hand at Dos Estrellas. He was hired on about the same time as the first horse theft."

Mel's interest was visibly piqued. "You think he's responsible?"

"Not really."

"How can you say that for certain?"

"I can't." Aaron polished off his sandwich with a swig of soda. "Except I doubt someone brand-new to the valley could pull off a series of sophisticated horse thefts that clearly require familiarity with the area. Especially a kid barely out of high school."

"He could be working with someone local. You said so yourself."

"Yeah. Maybe."

"Or he's savvier than you're giving him credit for."

Aaron laughed. "You missed your calling, Mel. You'd make a good detective. But you're right. I shouldn't discount the kid just because he's young and not the sharpest tack in the box."

"I wish there was something more I could do. I'd hate for another foal to lose his mama."

"Your little guy improving?"

"I thought he might have turned a corner, but then he barely ate today." She sighed. "He's literally going to die of loneliness if I can't come up with a miracle."

"Being orphaned is never easy on youngsters."

"I'm sorry." Mel's face fell. "That was thoughtless of me."

"Kaylee was just a few weeks old when Robin died. She doesn't remember her mother."

"She knows she doesn't have one. How can she not? All her friends do. The loss is there and may grow greater as she gets older."

"Nancy's wonderful with her. She really tries hard to fill the void."

"Anyone can see she adores Kaylee. I have a great respect for her."

"Look, about her confronting you earlier."

Mel blinked in surprise. "She told you?"

"A friend of hers saw us the other night at Vito's. Nancy's still sore."

"Is that why you haven't suggested getting together again?"

"Partly," he admitted.

Mel resumed eating her sandwich. "I figured it was something like that."

"Nancy can be a little pushy."

"She was actually very civil."

"But she got her point across, I bet."

"It's a valid point. She wants to protect Kaylee. And to protect Robin's memory."

"You aren't a threat to either, Mel."

She sought his gaze and held it for a long moment. "Aren't I?"

She was right. He'd been fooling himself all along, thinking he had a handle on his emotions. The proof he'd lost control was right here, staring him in the face and waiting for an answer.

"I shouldn't have left Kaylee with you. I apologize."

Mel turned away, perhaps to hide her disappointment in him. She'd bared her heart, gone out on a limb, and he hadn't had the decency to acknowledge her, much less open up in return. What was wrong with him? Why couldn't he admit he cared for her?

"I'm glad you did," she said. "Kaylee's a beautiful little girl. You're a lucky man."

"I am." He raised his hand to Mel's cheek, attempting to show her by his actions what he couldn't muster the courage to say. "In more ways than one."

She tilted her head away from his hand.

"Mel. I…" Dammit. Could he screw up any worse?

"I thought at Vito's, when we kissed, you might have feelings for me." She faltered. "Only then, you were distant. I understand now that might only be because of Nancy. But you should've said something."

"You're right." He balled up the foil from his sandwich and flung it into the ice chest. "I won't lie, coming to terms with having a baby, figuring out where we stand, it's not easy. For any of us. I'm doing my best."

"You have plenty of reason to be reluctant. That's not what frustrates me. You run hot and cold, Aaron. What am I supposed to think?"

Aaron took his time responding. "It's not that I've sworn off meeting someone special again or having more children. I just wasn't expecting it this soon."

"It's the same for me," Mel said softly. "I want children. Figured on having several. Someday. With a man who loves me."

The stab, intentional or not, hurt. Aaron

wanted to be that man, but first, he had to break the ties holding him to his past. Guilt kept preventing him.

"Have you told anyone about the baby besides Dolores?" he asked.

"Frankie."

"Was she happy for you?"

"Not really. Sort of." Mel made a face. "She was kind of funny. But she'll be supportive. She's a single mother, too."

Single mother. Mel was telling him in no uncertain terms she planned on raising their child alone.

"Also my dad," she added.

That took him aback. "How'd he handle it?"

"He'll be fine. And he promised not to shove his fist in your face."

"Oh, boy."

"I'm joking. He likes you. But he is worried about me."

"I would expect nothing else."

Aaron should be relieved, except he wasn't. Did Mel's family believe he wouldn't step up and take responsibility? Did she? He'd let her down. Multiple times. Who could blame her for not having faith in him? Add to that what Nancy had said to her today, and Mel's worst fears had probably been confirmed.

What he needed to do was reassure her. Words weren't his strong suit, as the last few minutes had demonstrated. There must be another way.

The answer was obvious and one Aaron should have thought of before. He started to speak, only to shut his mouth. This wasn't the time or place. Later, after he'd put some effort into preparing, he'd show Mel just how willing he was to step up.

"Samantha won today," Mel said. "Did you see?"

"Not her run. But I heard her name announced."

"There's a rodeo next weekend in Show Low. She's going."

"You, too?"

Mel shook her head. "Dad, Dolores and Ronnie will. I can't afford another day off."

"You need your rest," he reminded her.

"Did you see how hard we worked today? Helping Samantha compete is no vacation."

"How's her horse? Any improvement?" Aaron cleaned up their trash and the soda cans.

"It's a slow recovery. The tear was bad. She hopes he'll be well enough by the National Finals in December. I don't see that happening."

"She did win on your sister's horse."

"This competition was good practice for her and that horse. But Nationals is on a whole different level. Show Low will be make or break for her."

"Spoken like a big sister." Aaron worried he might have prodded a sore spot.

Evidently not, for Mel said, "She's not a bad kid. Just a bit mixed up. Like the rest of us, I suppose. Dolores thinks Samantha used the lottery money as an excuse to get to know us. I didn't agree with her at first. Now, I think she's right."

"It does make sense." Aaron rested a hand

on Mel's thigh, half waiting for her to smack it away.

Instead, she inched closer. He tried not to jump to any conclusions. Not easy. He very much liked the conclusions he was forming.

"Sam and I have a lot in common," Mel said, appearing unaware of Aaron's inner turmoil. "Have you ever noticed?"

Wait. Sam? Did Mel realize she'd called Samantha by the same nickname her father used? Those things in common must have formed a bond between them.

"I haven't. But I'm hoping you'll tell me."

"Her mom, Carrie Anne, she got involved with a man who wasn't emotionally available. That man being my dad."

"And you think I'm emotionally unavailable."

"Please." Mel turned to him, her eyes brimming with emotion. "I didn't mean that in a bad way. I'm simply trying to make sense of everything that's been happening lately."

"Me, too."

She touched his hand, her fingers light and

warm and sending tiny shock waves along his skin. "Somehow, we went from having this easy, comfortable relationship to one that's complicated and confusing. I'm not sure how that happened." She let out an uneven breath. "But I believe it's about more than just the baby."

Ah. Those feelings for her he wasn't ready to admit to having.

"I don't disagree with you." He pulled her nearer, securing her in the crook of his arm. "Whatever happens, we'll figure out a solution together. Trust me."

She nodded, swallowing before she spoke. "You're right."

Not that Aaron ever had much success in resisting Mel, but in that moment, she was so lovely and so vulnerable, resisting her wasn't an option.

"Aaron?" Her whispered question fell against his lips. "Are we only making things worse?"

He had to be honest with her. "I'd like to say no."

Convinced she'd pull away, he was elated when she raised her mouth to meet his.

Mel had called their relationship easy and comfortable. For Aaron, it had also been exciting and passionate. He believed Mel felt the same. Her eager response to his kiss certainly indicated as much.

Craving more contact, he drew her onto his lap. She came willingly, making him acutely aware of her enticing curves and firing his need.

Hooking a hand behind her knees, he repositioned her, the part of him most aware of her instantly responding. Mel slid her arms around his neck, parted her lips and kissed him with an intensity matched only by the summer heat.

In moments like this one, Aaron wasn't confused. In fact, he knew precisely what he wanted, and she was sitting in his lap.

One minute stretched into two. Two became five. The need driving Aaron grew, quickly approaching the point of no return.

Slowly, regretfully, he ended the kiss. "That was..." If he kept talking, he'd blabber like a fool.

Mel's arms fell away from him, and she cleared her throat. "We may have gotten carried away."

Aaron waited for his pounding heart to slow. "I'm not complaining."

"Me neither." And, yet, she stood, her damp shirt clinging to her skin and accentuating her hourglass shape. Grabbing her sunglasses, she moved away from him. "My family's waiting for me at Dad's."

"Right." Aaron also stood, not yet over the effects of their kiss. "If I hurry, I can tuck Kaylee into bed."

The parking area had completely emptied while they'd eaten and talked and done things bordering on indecent.

He took a chance and said, "Why don't we meet at the motel tomorrow?" That would allow him time to put his idea in motion.

"It hasn't been two weeks."

She couldn't be serious. Their usual routine had long gone by the wayside.

"I can't wait that long," he said.

She hesitated. "I'm not sure I'm ready to, you know, resume…"

"Just talk. Nothing more." Aaron tensed. This was the closest he'd come to making an admission. Did she not see that? "We can wait till later in the week if you want."

"Tomorrow's fine." She abruptly walked away, sending him a last, lingering glance over her shoulder. "Bye, Aaron."

He watched her until she reached her truck. Grabbing his cowboy hat and plunking it on his head, he shut the rear door of the SUV, all the while whistling to himself.

She hadn't exactly said yes. Then again, she hadn't exactly said no. Aaron was betting on the latter and would be at the motel tomorrow. Neither wild horses nor an irate mother-in-law would keep him away.

Chapter Eleven

Aaron was waiting for Mel in the parking area behind the motel. She spotted his SUV the moment she rounded the building. He must have seen her, too, for the driver's door opened, and he stepped out, cowboy boots and long legs first. He probably had no idea how great he looked. Aaron didn't spend any time trying to make an impression. He just did, naturally.

She briefly wondered why he chose the parking lot and not the room to wait for her. She was fifteen minutes late; he must've checked in already. His last text had said, "I'm here."

The space beside him was empty, and Mel parked there.

"Sorry I took so long. I was with the foal and lost track of time."

Aaron drew her into a quick, warm hug, catching her completely off guard. They didn't do that. Not in public.

"Is he okay?"

She needed a second to find her voice "I was worried he might have caught a respiratory infection, though he's not running a fever. I drew some blood to send to the lab tomorrow, just as a precaution."

"I'm glad you're here." He reached for her hand.

It was becoming a habit, this hand-holding. One she was growing to like. "Were you worried I wasn't coming?"

"Well, you were vague last night."

After that kiss they'd shared? How could he have had any doubts? That he did was interesting and, possibly, telling. Mel would revisit this recent development later at home.

"You check in already?" she asked.

He produced a key—an actual key, no plastic key cards at this motel. "Room 11."

Inside, he removed his wallet and two phones, tossing them onto the dresser. "I forgot water. Guess I was distracted."

"By work?" *Or thoughts of me?*

He stopped, letting his eyes roam over her. "That, too."

Mel's cheeks warmed. She reminded herself they were here to talk. Not tear each other's clothes off.

Aaron went to the dresser where a plastic ice bucket sat next to the coffeemaker. "Is tap water okay? I'll get some ice from the machine outside the lobby."

"I'm not picky."

She didn't offer to go with him. A minute alone would do her good. She'd been anxious about seeing Aaron since their make-out session in the rear of his SUV after the barrel-racing competition. There had been something so... so...regular-old-couple about it.

A sudden thought panicked her. What if she alone felt that way? Aaron's doubts about her showing up tonight indicated otherwise, but her confidence waned. She could be misreading him. She had before.

"Be right back." Aaron shut the door behind him.

Mel went to the window, parted the curtains and watched him disappear down the walkway. Exhaling slowly, she let the curtain drop back into place and returned to the dresser where she set her purse. Aaron's phone ringing startled her.

She glanced down, recognizing the blue phone as his personal one. Because he'd laid the phone with the screen down, she couldn't see who was calling. Nancy? Was Kaylee all right? Perhaps she should go after him. The ringing stopped and was eventually followed by a ping signaling a voice-mail message had been left.

Mel paced the room until Aaron returned twenty minutes later. Okay, really only five.

"You got a call while you were gone," she said

the instant he entered the room. "On your personal phone."

Handing her the ice bucket, he picked up the phone and swiped a finger across the screen. "It's my sister."

Mel was aware Aaron's sister knew about her and Aaron's arrangement. "Go ahead and call her back if you want."

"I won't be long."

While he listened to the voice-mail message, Mel removed two tumblers from the tray and added ice. Taking the glasses to the sink, she filled them with water. By then, Aaron was engrossed in conversation.

"Tell her I'll call tomorrow." After a pause, he said, "I can't tonight... Because I'm busy." Another pause. "Yeah, something like that."

Mel thought she might have heard a laugh coming from the phone and suffered a twinge of embarrassment.

"Love you, too, Pickle. Talk to you later." He disconnected, returning the phone to the dresser. "Mom's sick."

"Not seriously, I hope."

"Sounds like a bad summer cold. I'll call tomorrow."

"I'm sure she'll appreciate that." Mel just had to ask. "You call your sister Pickle?"

"A nickname from when we were kids. She hates it."

"Who wouldn't?"

Mel chewed her lip. She'd officially run out of excuses. With sex off the table, only conversation remained. This, she realized, would be the second time they'd come to the motel and refrained. In fact, they hadn't slept together since before she found out she was pregnant.

"Here's your water."

Before he could take the glass she offered, Mel's knees went boneless and her field of vision narrowed. The glass tumbler suddenly seemed to weigh twenty pounds and slipped from her fingers.

"Hey, hold on there!" Aaron materialized beside her. Taking her arm, he walked her across a floating room and eased her onto the side of the bed. "You okay?"

"Yeah." Mel closed her eyes, fighting the wave of dizziness and encroaching darkness. "No. I feel strange."

"Put your head between your legs."

She did. After a minute or so, the dizziness receded. As it did, she noticed Aaron had sat beside her, his arm securely around her shoulders.

"Careful," he warned when she tried to raise her head. "Go slow."

"I feel silly."

"Stop it." He rubbed her back, his palm making large circles. "Have you fainted before?"

"Not since I was six and the nurse gave me a shot."

"It's not uncommon. Especially in the first trimester. Your blood pressure could have spiked."

Had Robin fainted? Mel didn't ask.

"Here. Have some water." Aaron got up and retrieved her tumbler from the dresser. It was then Mel saw his tumbler on the floor, ice cubes spilled and laying atop a spreading wet spot.

"Did I do that?"

"It's just water. No harm done. The carpet will dry."

She rubbed her head, though the mild throbbing had mostly receded.

"Did you have dinner?" Aaron came back from the bathroom with a towel, which he used to blot the water.

"Yes. A chicken quesadilla and a salad, if you must know."

"Good girl."

He surprised Mel by arranging the pillows against the headboard and insisting she sit back and stretch out her legs.

"I'm fine. Really." She smiled. This was the most relaxed they'd been all evening.

"The dizziness usually doesn't last. Still, you might mention it to your doctor at your next visit. In fact, I insist you do if this happens again."

"Are you going to come with me and make sure I do?" she half joked.

"I'd like to. If you don't mind."

He was serious. And so sweet. She almost said yes. "What will Nancy say?"

"I'm telling her about the baby this week."

"That's not what I asked."

"Isn't it?"

He grinned, and the resulting zing winding through Mel had nothing to do with her earlier dizziness.

It didn't require a genius. Aaron's good looks were what had initially attracted Mel. But what kept her meeting him every two weeks for the last eight, no, nine, months was his *straightness*, for lack of a better word.

Simply put, Aaron was a straight up guy. What one saw was what one got. He was also straightforward. No beating around the bush. And he was a straight arrow. He held himself to high standards and did his best to adhere to those standards. Their affair might be his one and only fall from his pedestal. Ever.

He actually reminded Mel of her father, and not just because they had both lost a wife and wound up having a baby with a woman they didn't marry. They shared many good, admirable traits that had probably enhanced his attractiveness.

"You look serious," Aaron said. He still sat beside her on the bed. "What's wrong?"

"I was thinking about my dad." Not a lie, though not entirely accurate.

He laughed and tucked a loose strand of hair behind her ear. Another sweet gesture. "Not what I expected you to say."

"I was unfair to him when Samantha first showed up. Not that I agree with his decision to waive his parental rights. I've learned a lot these last couple weeks. People deal with grief differently. If seeing Carrie Anne helped him through a difficult time, then where's the harm? Again, other than their truly terrible choices regarding Samantha." Mel touched her belly. "I'll never understand that."

"They're a lot like us."

"Kind of. Only you aren't walking away from our child."

"And you're not insisting I do."

"Does that make us better than Dad and Carrie Anne? Samantha has a good life, even if she's currently at odds with her parents. Despite our best efforts, things could turn out badly for our child."

"I'm not going to let that happen, Mel."

There he was, taking her hand again.

"I apologized to Dad yesterday, before I told him about the baby."

"And the rest of your family?"

"I'm getting to them one by one." She gave him a look. "How about we make a pact? You tell Nancy this week, and I'll tell the rest of my family." She extended her hand for him to shake.

"Deal." He folded her fingers inside his. "I'd like to speak to them, too, if you don't mind."

That took her aback. "Why?"

"I want them to know I'm not abandoning you, and I won't be waiving my rights. Not for anything."

"I'm glad. I'd like our child to grow up with you loving him or her the way you love Kaylee."

"I already do." He raised her hand to his lips, brushed them lightly over her knuckles. "I'm not unhappy at the prospect of spending the next twenty years with you. And not just because of the baby."

In that instant, she knew what she felt for Aaron had gone far past affection and attraction. If he didn't reciprocate, she was heading straight for heartache.

She should get off the bed. Leave. Run away. Before she did something stupid. Something she couldn't take back.

Only Mel stayed put, studying their clasped hands. They'd been flirting a lot lately. He'd given her a hug outside. They'd kissed as if they couldn't get enough of each other. His feelings for her *must* be deepening.

Maybe if she let him know in no uncertain terms she was ready to go from casual to committed, he'd tell her that was what he wanted, too.

Only one way to find out, right?

Mel reached up and cradled Aaron's cheek, brought his mouth to hers.

He resisted.

Mel withdrew, mortified. Clearly, she'd made a mistake. He didn't want her. Not like that.

He brought her gaze back to his and stopped her from looking away when she tried. "Mel, listen. I can't let you start anything you aren't prepared to finish. I want you too much."

Excitement spiraled through her. Hot. Electric. Powerful.

It wasn't enough, however. She needed more.

"This isn't just sex for me, Aaron. Not anymore."

"Me neither." Taking her by the shoulders, he lowered his mouth to hers. "I couldn't bear to hurt you. If there's any chance of that happening, tell me to go, and I will."

"Stay."

Mel leaned back against the pillows, bringing him with her. This time, he didn't resist.

THIS WASN'T WHAT Aaron had planned when he suggested meeting Mel at the motel tonight. Kissing her. Holding her in his arms. Needing her to cling to him and cry his name as he entered her.

No. He'd wanted to talk. And to ask her...

She nipped at his ear, and his mind shut down.

Mel could do that. Make him forget everything, including his own name.

"Wait." She sat up and wriggled back a bit.

He groaned. Had she come to her senses? It seemed yes, which was probably for the best.

"Give me a minute to recover," he grumbled.

"I'll give you two seconds to prepare."

"Huh?"

In one quick, efficient move, she removed her shirt, slipping it over her head and flinging it onto the floor.

"There."

Aaron stared, lost in the sight before him. She was gorgeous. Her normally satiny skin glowed. And her breasts, rounded to begin with, spilled from the tops of her turquoise bra.

He couldn't keep from touching her and reveled in her low, dreamy sigh when he slid the straps down, taking care to smooth his hand over the silky curve of her exposed shoulders.

She leaned forward, reached behind her and unfastened the hooks. The bra instantly fell away, freeing her and revealing every stunning inch of her.

His throat went bone-dry.

"Are you sure about this? You were feeling faint earlier."

"Don't worry. I'm not getting up." Letting the bra fall onto the floor, she scooted over, making more room for him on the bed. "I'm planning on staying in bed for the next hour at least." When he didn't move, she sent him a seductive smile. "That is, if you'll join me."

Her playful tone and manner reminded him of how they'd been before they found out about the baby, as if the past few stress-filled weeks hadn't happened. Aaron struggled to hold back, determined not to climb all over her like some inexperienced teenager. No matter what, they were going slow—until going slow was no longer possible.

He kicked off his boots, which hit the floor with a thud, landing in the vicinity of her bra. Next, he stood and divested himself of his shirt, jeans and the remainder of his clothes. Mel watched, her eyes never straying. He, in turn, watched her. By the time he removed his underwear, he was hard and ready.

Rather than fall onto the bed beside her, he reached for her sandals and slipped them off. Her toes were painted with a bright blue polish. Cute. When she ran her toes in a swirly pattern down the length of his chest to his stomach, then lower, he was thinking blue was his new favorite color.

Her shorts were next. The sound of fabric against skin when they glided over her hips nearly did him in. Finally, Mel lay naked in front of him, the dainty scrap of fabric she dared to call her panties dangling from his fingers.

Lying there, completely unabashed, she took his breath away. And his ability to move. The panties, as light as a feather, drifted to the floor.

Curling onto her side, she drew circles on the hideous floral bedspread. "You're wasting time, cowboy."

Nothing sexier than a direct woman.

Aaron lay down beside her and scooped her into his arms. When she made a small sound of protest, he froze. "You all right?"

"I'm a little tender." She indicated her breasts.

Concerned, he drew back. "We should stop."

"Absolutely not."

"You're in pain."

She pushed him down onto his back and swung a leg over his middle. "I won't be if I'm on top."

Before he could answer, she straddled him and braced her arms on each side of his head. Those magnificent, if tender, breasts were within kissing distance. On her face, she wore a wicked smile.

"See? I knew we could find a solution."

No reason for him to worry. She seemed completely recovered from her fainting spell.

"Make love to me, Aaron."

Make love. Not have sex. Not hook up. Not fool around. Had either of them ever said "made love" before? Aaron didn't think so.

"I have every intention of doing that and more." He skimmed his palms down her back, over her smooth, rounded hips and along her thighs.

"More? I'm intrigued. Describe this *more* to me." She rocked back and forth. Side to side.

He sucked in a sharp breath. "I'd rather show you."

Grabbing the backs of her knees, he moved her legs until she was poised in the perfect position. When she reached for him, he told her to wait.

"There's more. Remember?"

She pressed her forehead to his and murmured, "Quit teasing me."

Aaron proceeded to make good on his promise. Dragging her mouth down for a kiss, he slipped his hand between her legs, excited as always to find her ready for him.

He'd made a point from the very beginning

to learn what she liked. Which way, how much pressure to apply, where her most sensitive spots were, when to go faster, when to let her take the lead. That last one was the most important for it almost always guaranteed her satisfaction.

He had no problem giving up control. *His* satisfaction was also something Mel liked, and she had a talent for finding new and different ways to excite him. And herself.

"Like that," she whispered when he entered her. "Don't stop."

Aaron didn't. Not until they were both covered in sweat and completely sated.

She fell forward and buried her head in his neck, a low moan escaping. He kissed her cheek and temple and that place behind her ear, noticing the faint flowery scent of her shampoo.

"Aaron?"

"Mmm?"

"That was…" She moaned again.

"I'll say."

Eventually, when their strength returned, she rolled off him and onto the mattress. He groaned, from the rush of cool air and the abrupt loss of contact, not his aching muscles.

"I've missed you."

She propped herself up on an elbow and peered at him. "Me, or the sex? Because we just saw each other yesterday."

"I've missed the closeness."

"We were pretty close in your SUV yesterday, as I recall."

"I'm not good at expressing myself." He chuckled and tweaked her cheek. "And you don't make it any easier."

She rolled over onto her back, her smile flatlining.

"Did I say something wrong?"

"If I ask you a question, will you answer honestly?"

He levered himself up, to look at her and also to assure her he was taking this conversation seriously. "Absolutely."

"You said you liked the idea of spending the next twenty years with me raising our child."

"I did. I can't wait."

"How do you want to spend those twenty years? Have you given it any thought?"

"Actually, I have." He spoke slowly, fearing he might say the wrong thing or that he hadn't understood her question. Was she referring to the sex? To them and the baby? Maybe he shouldn't have said twenty years.

She stared at the ceiling as if avoiding him. This was going from bad to worse.

"Look at me, Mel."

She faced him, her eyes filled with sadness. When had her mood changed and why?

"I'm sorry," she said.

"For what?"

"I put you on the spot again. That wasn't fair."

"After what just happened between us, which, let's admit was mind-blowing, it's more than fair. We deserve to know where we stand with each other."

"I agree. So, tell me, where do I stand?"

Shit. This wasn't going the way Aaron had planned. But it would have to do.

Pointing a finger at her, he said, "Hold that thought."

"You're kidding." She didn't sound amused.

Aaron sat up and reached for his jeans on the floor. From the front pocket, he pulled out a small velvet jewelry box.

This morning, he'd gone into Scottsdale and made a purchase. Taking Kaylee with him, he'd let her help pick out the ring, though he hadn't told her who it was for and why. A stop for ice-cream cones had secured a promise from her not to tell her grandmother or anyone else.

Straightening, he held out the box to Mel, opening the lid to display the object inside. "I was saving this for later. Thought I might get down on one knee. The whole nine yards." He grinned, more than a little pleased with himself. "Mel, will you—"

"No." She snatched the bedsheet with one hand and covered herself. She held up her other hand as if to ward him off. "Don't."

"I'm asking you to—"

"I know *what* you're asking. What I want to know is *why*?"

He frowned. "Why I want to marry you?"

"It's a reasonable question, Aaron."

He supposed it was. He hadn't made any flowery speeches or broken down with unrestrained emotion. Hadn't given her reason to believe no one in the world mattered more to him than she did and that he couldn't spend another day without her by his side. He hadn't said he loved her.

When he tried, the words stuck in his throat. Not just because of Robin or any sense of loyalty to her. And not because Mel wasn't someone he *could* love. Eventually. She'd be a wonderful wife and partner, and a great stepmom to Kaylee.

But that wasn't what she'd want to hear, either.

Aaron closed his eyes. He took admissions of love very seriously and believed Mel did, too. She'd instantly dismiss empty platitudes or insincere declarations, rightfully tossing them back in his face.

"I like the idea of us marrying and raising our family together. You're someone I want to be with. Someone I clearly care for. I think I can make you happy. I know you'll make me happy."

She shook her head, and when she spoke, tears clogged her voice.

"Not good enough."

"Mel. Please."

She climbed out of bed and went straight for her clothes. Shoving her arms into the sleeves of her shirt, she quickly dressed.

"Mel. Hang on." Aaron found his underwear among the remaining scattered clothes and stepped into them. "Where are you going?"

"Home. To check on the foal. Frankie's. I'm not sure."

"Wait." Pocketing the ring box, he finished dressing. "We're not done talking."

"I think we are." She began gathering her things. Purse. Cell phone. Sandals.

Aaron realized he had less than twenty seconds to change Mel's mind and stop her from leaving. Whatever he said next, it had to be good.

Chapter Twelve

*I love you. You are every woman I've ever de-
sired rolled into one. Marry me and make me
the happiest man alive.*

Or, words to that effect. Mel wasn't particular.
As long as Aaron mentioned love and looked
at her with a besotted expression on his face.

The same besotted expression he wore when
he talked about his late wife.

Mel refused to be an afterthought or a conse-
quence of duty or a means of avoiding a messy
custody battle. She'd rather raise her child alone
and without a red cent from him.

"I botched the proposal." Aaron reached around and prevented her hand from opening the door.

She didn't think he'd forcibly detain her. He wasn't the type.

"I could have done a better job."

"You think?" Okay, she was being snippy. But when did proposing become a job?

Mel frowned. Why was she not hightailing it to her truck? She supposed some part of her wanted to hear what Aaron had to say. Feel that he recognized and understood how much he'd hurt her.

"Let me try again," he said.

She turned, thinking he couldn't be serious. "You're asking for a do over?"

He continued as if he hadn't heard her. "I want to give you and our child the best home possible. Is that wrong?"

"Being married is no guarantee."

"Call me old-fashioned. I like the idea of a traditional family."

Kudos to Frankie, she'd pegged Aaron 100 percent.

Something her father had said the night Samantha showed up suddenly came to Mel. He'd proposed to Carrie Anne out of duty. Not love. Aaron's reasons for proposing to Mel were too similar, wounding her even greater.

She stole her sister's favorite quote, more resolved than ever to stand her ground. "One happy parent is better than two miserable parents."

"What if we aren't miserable?"

"Marriage is hard. Even for couples in love." More wise words from Frankie.

"Kaylee likes you," Aaron said, trying a different tactic.

"And I like her," Mel said. "But what about Nancy? Would she be part of our *traditional family*?"

"I doubt she'd stay with us. She'll probably get a place of her own nearby."

"You doubt it? Does that mean you won't ask her to leave?"

He waited a fraction too long before answering. "I will."

"If it comes to that. But you'd rather not. Which makes me out to be a bitch. Nicely done, Aaron."

It was silly for them to continue standing at the door. Mel, however, wasn't budging. Aaron needed to think she might flee any second.

"You're right," he admitted. "Nancy would be crushed, and I'd hate hurting her."

"But not me?"

"Yes, you." Everything about him screamed defeat. From his untucked shirt to his shoeless feet and mussed hair. "I didn't think this through before I went and bought the ring."

She didn't tell him the ring and his spontaneous purchase of it was the only romantic part in all this wretchedness. The solitaire diamond nestled in a circle of smaller diamonds was beautiful and exactly the kind of ring Mel would have picked out herself.

"I really do understand your loyalty to Nancy," she said. "She's an important part of Kaylee's

life. Of your life. I would have always respected
that and accommodated her."

"Would have?"

A sharp pain speared Mel's chest. The effect
of having her heart broken.

How could she have not realized the enormity of her feelings for Aaron? Fear of rejection,
most likely. So what did she do? She walked
the wobbly limb of baring souls all by her lone-
some. Gee, and look where it got her.

"I'll accept child support," she said. "Only
because I won't deprive our child. And you can
see him or her as much as you want. We'll come
up with a reasonable schedule that works for
both of us."

"Dammit, Mel."

"I think I'm being very accommodating."

"Except now I'm feeling cornered."

Was he not listening to a thing she said?
"None of this is my fault."

"That's not entirely true."

She stiffened. "If you're feeling cornered, it's

because you painted yourself into one by pro-posing."

"You're the one who insisted on dissecting my remark about twenty years."

"Dissecting? *Dissecting?* Excuse me for try-ing to understand your intentions."

"Are you sure you weren't trying to force me to—"

"That's it. This discussion is officially over."

He struggled for composure. "Sorry. Wrong word choice."

Not that excuse again. "Goodbye, Aaron."

"I'm upset. You're upset." He put a hand on her arm. "Let's meet tomorrow, after we've both had a chance to cool off."

If not for the fact he didn't seem to realize how much he'd hurt her, she'd agree. "I can't. I'm busy."

"Then when are you free?"

She took a breath and reached for the door-knob. "I'll let you know."

"I hate that things have come to this point." Regret filled his eyes.

"It was bound to happen. We made a mistake. We thought we could sleep together, no strings attached. Without falling for each other. Then, despite developing feelings anyway, despite this baby being a very big string attaching us, we kept trying to play by the old rules."

"Have you fallen for me?"

How like a guy to hear only one thing.

"That doesn't matter now. We got in over our heads. Way over." She had to hurry before her worst nightmare came true, and she started crying. She was already on the verge. "You want to do right by me and the baby. I want a man who loves me the way you loved Robin." There, she'd said it.

"Give me time."

"Time? This isn't some TV sitcom where the star finally falls for the quirky neighbor after three seasons. You either love somebody or you don't."

Their conversation had circled an empty track for the last time. Even if Aaron dropped to his knees and begged her, she wouldn't marry him.

She wrenched opened the door.

He must've decided any further pleas would fall on deaf ears because he didn't stop her.

As she crossed the threshold, she felt the faintest of brushes on her arm. It might have been Aaron's hand. Or, the air conditioning turning on.

She half walked, half ran down the path. Her blinking truck lights, normally welcoming, seemed to mock her.

Mel swore when the key wouldn't fit in the ignition. After several frustrating failed attempts, she stopped, inhaled and tried again, willing her fingers to cease their trembling. If she didn't get out of here soon, Aaron would come walking around the corner.

Finally, thank God, the key went in, and she started for home. At the last minute, Mel changed her mind and headed to Frankie's house. She needed to talk to someone, and she'd rather that someone already know about Aaron and the baby.

She must've looked terrible for Frankie uttered, "Are you okay?" the moment she opened the door.

The emotion Mel had been holding in for the last twenty minutes burst free. Sobbing, she threw herself at her sister.

Frankie gasped. "Is the baby all right?"

"Aaron and I broke up."

"I thought you weren't dating."

"Not funny."

"Who's joking?"

Patting Mel's back, she maneuvered them to the couch. At this hour, the girls were fast asleep. Mel and Frankie could talk privately.

"Sit. I'll make us some hot tea."

How like her older sister, convinced tea was the universal cure for whatever ailed a person.

"I don't want any."

"All right." She reclined against the cushions. "Tell me what happened."

"He proposed."

"I thought you said you broke up."

"We did. He had a ring. I told him no before

he could finish. And to answer the question I see burning in your eyes, he doesn't love me."

"Are you sure? He did propose."

Mel recalled Aaron's expression when he'd produced the ring box. He'd been wearing a goofy, didn't-I-do-good grin like her nieces did when they made a macaroni-and-construction-paper Christmas ornaments.

"I'm sure," Mel said.

"He was willing to do the right thing. That counts for a lot. It shows he's a decent guy."

"He is a decent guy. But me being pregnant isn't reason enough to get married."

"You have to consider your child."

"I am. Lots of single parents raise happy and healthy kids. Look at you."

"Maybe I'm not the best role model. Children do need a father."

Mel started crying again. "I want my husband to be in love with me."

"We all want that, honey. But I'm not sure it's possible."

"What's wrong with us?" Mel lamented.

"Bad timing, I guess. Bad choices."

"I think if I had met Aaron a couple years from now, we'd be dating."

"Possibly. But what good does playing that kind of game accomplish? Other than making yourself feel worse?"

Her sister was right.

"I really wanted things to work out with Aaron. I've never admitted that before. Not to myself, not to anyone."

Frankie put an arm around Mel. "Are you in love with him?"

"I might be. Yes, a little. I think so." She sniffed. "Not that it matters. I screwed up."

"Been there, done that." Frankie's tone had the ring of personal experience.

"I shouldn't have gotten mad."

"He hurt you. Anger is a natural defense."

"What am I going to do?"

"About what?" Frankie asked. "The baby? Aaron? The fact you're clearly in love with him?"

"All of the above?"

Frankie became instantly pragmatic. It was how she dealt with life's blows. She'd done it when Samantha appeared at their father's birthday party and when Spence left, forcing her to raise their two daughters on her own.

"About the baby, you and Aaron will talk. Once you've had some time to think. About Aaron, you'll get along with him because it's best for everyone involved. About being in love with him, he'll own a small piece of your heart forever."

"Like his late wife owns a small piece of his," Mel said glumly.

"Look. If you're not going to marry him, then hire my attorney and get yourself an airtight custody agreement. You don't want him taking your baby from you."

Was that what Frankie feared? Spence returning and wanting custody of their daughters?

"Aaron wouldn't do that."

"A legal contract will make sure he doesn't."

What strength Mel had left seeped slowly out of her. She'd just turned down a proposal from a wonderful man any woman would be thrilled to marry. She still believed her reasons were good, but doubts were starting to creep in and take hold.

She stood. "I should get home."

"Are you okay to drive?"

"I'll be fine."

Frankie walked her to the door. "Call me anytime. Day or night. I don't care." They hugged. "Love you, honey."

Mel went outside. Once removed from Frankie's calming influence, her anger returned. Not at Aaron but at herself. She'd walked eyes wide open into a situation that couldn't possibly end well. Stupid, stupid, stupid.

Starting tomorrow, she was making a new plan, one based entirely on logic and without emotion. One that made her baby a priority. And she'd stick to the plan, come hell or high water. No breaking the rules just because some sexy cowboy came along who turned her head and awakened her long slumbering libido.

She'd learned her lesson, thank you very much. Love was for dreamers and people with their heads in the clouds.

Not her. Not again.

AARON HAD ONLY been to Dos Estrellas Ranch once before, and it wasn't on business. Though he didn't know the Dempseys well, he'd been invited to the wedding reception for Josh, the oldest of the three brothers who owned the ranch, and Cara, the manager of the mustang sanctuary.

Of course, half the town had been invited to the reception. He supposed no one wanted to exclude the local deputy.

This time the reason for his visit was official. He'd just completed a lengthy interview with Mike O'Donnald, the young, newly hired ranch hand who'd come under suspicion related to the recent spate of horse thefts.

Initially, Aaron had dismissed the kid as an unlikely suspect. But, then, he'd heard a second rumor and was compelled to follow up. After nearly two hours, he was leaving the ranch with the same opinion as before. Mike wasn't their man. Or, teenager in this case. Besides his alibis checking out, he simply didn't strike Aaron as the type to steal horses. An aw-shucks personality like his couldn't be faked.

Aaron tended to blame the rumors on folks being scared enough to point fingers without thinking. Mike was new to the community and had admitted when hired at Dos Estrellas that his dad was currently in prison, serving time for stealing a car.

The interview had been Aaron's last call in what had turned out to be a long, grueling day. Shortly after coming on duty, he'd been dispatched to break up two neighbors exchanging verbal blows over the placement of a fence. He'd hardly finished with them when he was summoned to the local market to arrest a shoplifter—who turned out to be a scared seven-year-old unable to stop crying. Before going to Dos Estrellas, he'd written three tickets for illegally parked cars. In this heat, no one wanted to walk one block farther than necessary.

Being busy wasn't all bad. It did give him a few minutes reprieve here and there from thinking about Mel.

Damn, he missed her. More than two weeks had passed since their night at the motel when they'd gone from making incredible love, to his rejected marriage proposal, to ending things completely and not seeing each other at all.

They kept in regular contact though. He made sure she was eating right, getting enough rest and that she knew without a doubt he'd help in whatever way she needed. He'd asked to tag along at her next doctor appointment, and she'd agreed, if hesitantly.

Their conversations were always polite and sometimes bordered on nice. Aaron wondered if someone else was in the room during those calls. Like her sisters or Dolores.

As he cruised the road from the ranch to town, tired, grouchy and hungry, he tried to pinpoint exactly when Mel had gotten under his skin, though that hardly described his feelings for her. Not right away, for sure. He'd been too cautious to let anyone in, too convinced he was making a mistake.

What had Mel said about falling in love? You either did or you didn't.

To him, she was like an addiction that started out as an occasional indulgence. Before long, he couldn't go a day without seeing or hearing from her.

Was that love? Aaron didn't know. The only woman he'd loved was Robin, and their relationship had taken an entirely different course than his and Mel's.

Aaron rubbed his temple. He'd been nursing a headache off and on for days. Sixteen days to be precise.

A chime from his personal cell phone distracted him. He was startled, then alarmed, to see Frankie's number. Was she calling about Mel?

"Hi, Frankie," he said with forced calm. Mel's sister knew the story. By now, her entire family had been told about her pregnancy and former relationship with Aaron. He had no idea what they thought, not having talked to them since his falling out with Mel. "What's up?"

"Just wondering if you're busy tomorrow. The girls have been begging me to invite Kaylee over for another playdate. Thought I'd give you a call and ask if you're free."

"We are. And I'm sure Kaylee would love to come over. What time and what can I bring?"

"Kid snacks, if you're inclined. And be sure Kaylee doesn't forget her swimsuit. Also, there's something else…"

Forget being calm. "Is it Mel? Tell me."

"No, she's fine. Stubborn. What else is new?"

Interesting. This was the first time Frankie had dropped a hint of how she felt about Mel and Aaron's breakup.

"We recently took in a stray puppy," Frankie said. "About three months old. He's really cute and superfriendly, if a bit excitable. Perfect size for a kid. Half Chihuahua and half terrier. Kaylee always loves playing with the animals when she comes over. I thought she might want a dog of her own."

Aaron liked pets. Robin had owned a clownish yellow Lab when they married. Unable to care for a dog and a brand-new baby in the wake of Robin's death, Aaron had given the dog to his parents, who still owned him.

He always thought of getting another pet when Kaylee was older. A puppy might make a perfect early birthday present.

"Sure."

"Really?" Frankie's voice rose with delight.

"We could use a positive change in the house."

"I'm sorry." There was no need to ask what or who she was referring to.

"Me, too."

They discussed a few more playdate details before disconnecting. Aaron contemplated how he'd break the news of the puppy to Nancy. She might not be too pleased, having to watch a puppy while he was at work. But she'd liked Robin's Lab and would do anything for Kaylee, so maybe he was anticipating a problem where there wasn't one.

Passing through the center of town, Aaron decided to stop at the feed store. They stocked a small inventory of pet supplies, including dog and cat food. Might be a good idea to have a bag of puppy chow on hand before tomorrow.

A bell over the door announced his arrival. Glancing at the wall clock, the face of which advertised a popular grain supplier, he calculated he had about fifteen minutes before closing time.

"Howdy." He nodded at the assistant manager behind the counter, trying to recall her name.

"Be right with you."

She was waiting on another customer. The middle-aged man in dusty boots and an old T-shirt leaned casually against the counter, giving the impression he was a frequent and welcome visitor to the store. But Aaron immediately picked up a negative vibe from him, which could be because he and the manager had been caught socializing when she should be working.

"Where's the dog food?" Aaron asked.

"First aisle on the left." Her smile appeared strained.

Aaron didn't think much of it. Uniforms intimidated some people, even innocent ones.

Looking over the available supply of puppy chow, Aaron selected a small bag, along with matching water and food bowls. He and Kaylee could make a trip later in the week to the pet-supply store in Scottsdale for a collar and leash and anything else they needed.

Did Mel treat small animals? Should he ask her to give the puppy its vaccinations and a checkup?

By the time Aaron carried his purchases to the counter, the other man had left. The assistant manager stared out the large window, but not at her friend. Ray Hartman had arrived and was climbing out of his truck.

The assistant manager shot Aaron a glance. Evidently, she and the entire town now knew about Mel and Aaron. The assistant manager must be worried he and Ray were going to have a showdown.

Aaron didn't duck and he didn't hide. He was going to be a part of Mel's life for a very long time. He intended to get along with each and every member of her family.

Setting the puppy chow and dishes on the counter, he reached for his wallet. While the assistant manager checked him out, Ray entered the store. He spotted Aaron immediately.

Glancing at Aaron's purchases, he smiled. "I thought you might be here on a call. Apparently not."

"It seems Kaylee is getting a new puppy courtesy of Frankie."

"Ah. That one." He shook his head. "Always rescuing some stray."

Not only was their exchange civil, it was downright sociable.

The assistant manager completed the transaction and handed Aaron his change and receipt. "Thanks for coming in."

He grabbed his purchases and, rather than

leave, walked over to Ray, who was reading the notices on the bulletin board. "I'm not sure what Mel has told you, sir."

His smile returned. "She's having a baby. I'm going to be a grandfather again. And you're the dad."

That about summed it up. "I wanted you to know, I'm going to support the baby and share in raising him or her." He considered mentioning to Ray that he'd proposed but decided against it.

"Mighty admirable of you."

Aaron almost asked Ray to repeat himself. Had he heard correctly? It sounded as if the older man wasn't angry. Hard to believe. If Aaron was confronting the father of his precious daughter's baby, he'd have a few choice words to say if nothing else.

"You aren't leaving Mel in the lurch," Ray said. "I give you credit for that. Wish I'd done the same with Samantha." Ray held out his hand for Aaron to shake. "We're going to see a lot of each other from now on. No reason we can't get along."

"I couldn't agree more, sir." Aaron accepted Ray's hand, impressed by the older man's firm grip.

"I figure any man Mel takes a liking to can't be all bad."

Aaron chuckled mirthlessly. "Did take a liking to."

"Did. Does." Ray gave Aaron a clap on the shoulder. "I'd best finish my shopping before the store closes. Dolores has dinner waiting for me."

The assistant manager seemed relieved when Aaron left.

He barely noticed, unable to get the encounter with Ray out of his head. The man's attitude was unexpected. But what had Aaron replaying the scene over and over in his head was Ray's remark about Mel.

Did...*does*? Was it possible she still cared? And how did Aaron find out?

Chapter Thirteen

Kaylee greeted Aaron the second he walked through the door, crashing into him and hugging his knees.

"Daddy, Daddy!"

He lifted her into his arms, and she rewarded him with a wet, sticky kiss on the cheek. Not that he minded.

"You're home," Nancy said from the kitchen. She stood at the counter, cutting up tomatoes for a salad. She and Kaylee usually ate earlier, and Aaron had leftovers.

"I have a surprise for you." Aaron tickled

Kaylee's neck before putting her down. "Two, actually."

"What? Tell me."

"Paige and Sienna's mom invited you over tomorrow. After lunch."

"Yay!" Kaylee jumped up and down in excitement. She'd just seen her little friends at preschool that day. Apparently, that wasn't enough time together.

"And, if you want, she has a puppy for us!"

Kaylee's face brightened as if she'd swallowed a ray of sunshine. "A puppy! For me?"

"We have to see him first, then decide if we want him."

Kaylee had already made up her mind for she ran to her grandmother and shouted, "Gramma, I'm getting a puppy."

"I heard." Nancy wiped her hands on a dish towel, and then tossed the towel onto the counter. "Shouldn't we talk about this first?"

"Okay." Aaron went over to the table, pulled out a chair and sat. A plate and silverware was already set out for him. "Let's talk."

He'd mostly made up his mind. But letting Nancy have a say in the decision might improve her willingness to cooperate.

"A puppy requires a tremendous amount of attention." She joined him at the table.

"I know I'm asking a lot from you. I'll help as much as possible. And Kaylee can take on some responsibility."

Nancy looked skeptical. "A three-year-old?"

Aaron inhaled slowly. Getting mad would gain nothing. "Please, Nancy. I'd really like to get her this puppy. She could use a boost. We've all been a little out of sorts lately."

"We? I'd say you're the only one in a bad mood."

"Daddy," Kaylee interrupted. "Can the puppy sleep in my room?"

"Sure. But you'll have to make a bed for him."

Kaylee hurried off, presumably to her room to construct a puppy bed. Just as well. Aaron preferred she not hear his conversation with Nancy.

"I didn't realize my mood was affecting everyone." He'd been trying hard to put forth a pleasant—if not happy—face.

"Don't get me wrong," Nancy said. "I'm glad you aren't seeing that woman anymore."

That woman? Her tone rubbed him the wrong way. "Her name is Mel."

Nancy ignored his remark. "Are you sure taking Kaylee tomorrow is a good idea? What if she's there again?"

She? Aaron was definitely getting tired of this. "Just in case I wasn't clear earlier, you should know I really care about Mel. She's more than a friend."

"I see." Nancy drew herself up. "I wonder what Robin would have thought of her?"

"She was one of the most practical, and generous, people I've ever met. She told me before she died that she wanted me to be open to finding someone new someday."

"Is Mel that someone new?"

She might have been. Regretfully, Aaron had blown his chances with her before finding out.

"She's important to me. And she's going to remain important for a long, long time."

He was yet to tell Nancy about Mel's pregnancy. Yes, he should have done so before now, but he hadn't wanted to deal with her reaction. Not while he was still coping, apparently poorly, with his and Mel's breakup.

"She's having a baby. My baby." Aaron spoke quickly, as if that would soften the blow. "I'm going to be an involved parent, and Kaylee will be an involved sister."

Nancy went stone still. For a full minute.

"I understand you're upset," Aaron finally said.

"Actually, I don't think you understand me at all." She stood and clasped her hands, but not before he noticed the tremor. "I'll need a few weeks."

"For what?"

"To move out."

"Sit down, Nancy," Aaron said gently. "You're not moving."

"Clearly, you've started a new life and don't need me."

He had always given Nancy a lot of leeway, making allowances for her immeasurable grief. But this threat to move, like all her previous threats, was a way of manipulating him. He'd let her get away with it for too long, choosing the path of least resistance instead of standing up to her.

Not anymore.

"Forget it," he said. "I've changed my mind. Go on and move if that's what you want."

She stared at him, the bluster draining from her like air escaping a punctured inner tube.

"I won't stop you," he continued. "Kaylee will be heartbroken, of course, but you need to do what you need to do."

"You can't be serious."

"I'm not abandoning Mel and our baby. If you're unable to accept that, or can't bear the thought of it, then I'll respect your wish to leave. You're always welcome to visit and stay as long as you like."

"What will you do with Kaylee? Who will watch her?"

"I'll figure something out. Hire a babysitter. Enroll her in day care."

Nancy slowly lowered herself into her seat.

After a moment, Aaron said with a smile, "That's better."

"I'm not sure what you're insinuating."

"Nancy, you're part of this family. An important, irreplaceable part. And not just because you watch Kaylee while I'm at work. You're her grandmother. Her one real connection, besides me, to her mother. Don't let your anger at me rob Kaylee of your love and guidance."

"What happens to me if you do…find someone new? Or, decide you want to marry Mel Hartman? Another woman isn't going to want her husband's former mother-in-law living with them."

This, Aaron suspected, was the real reason Nancy clung to the past and insisted he did, too. She was scared that, with Robin gone, and without Aaron and Kaylee, she'd lose her place in the world and never find it again.

His anger and frustration at her vanished. "If whoever this woman turns out to be can't accept you, then maybe she's not the right person for me."

"You say that now."

"There may come a day when you move out and have your own home. Not just because it's more comfortable for me. But because you're ready. I really hope that home is near Kaylee and me."

Blinking away a tear, she rose. "I'd better get your dinner on the table. You must be hungry."

This time, Aaron didn't stop her.

Nancy wasn't the demonstrative type. She didn't hug. She didn't make emotional declarations. In her subtle way, she was accepting what Aaron said and apologizing to him. It was, perhaps, her first step in facing a future that didn't revolve entirely around him and Kaylee.

If only he and Mel had been able to resolve their problems so easily. How different their last evening at the motel would have gone. He might be sitting across from her instead of Nancy, talking about a puppy for their brand new family.

He wasn't done trying with Mel, not after what Ray had said in the feed store. The problem was she'd yet to give any indication the wall she'd erected to keep him at bay could be breached. Until then, Aaron didn't stand a chance.

His personal cell phone went off, startling him. The ringtone identified the caller as Mel, giving him an even greater start. Pushing back from the table, he dived for the phone on the counter.

"Hi." He strove to sound casual. "What's going on?"

"I'm at The Small Change," she blurted. "With the orphan foal. Something's going on here. I think the horse thieves are back. I noticed a strange truck and trailer cutting across the back of the outbuildings toward the gate."

"Where does the gate lead?"

"To the cattle-grazing sections. But the mustang sanctuary is there, too."

Aaron glanced at the kitchen clock. It was past seven thirty and well into dusk. Night would be falling soon. Mel didn't need to be at the stables in the dark and with potentially dangerous individuals in the vicinity.

"You get out of there, you hear me?" Aaron all but shouted into the phone.

"I can't. The foal's sick. He must've ingested some moldy hay or pellets. I'm really worried about him."

"His life isn't worth yours, Mel. If the thieves are there and they think you've spotted them, you could be in real trouble."

"Aaron—"

He cut her off. "Get in your truck, lock the doors and crouch down. Don't go anywhere. If they see your lights, they'll figure out they've been spotted. Do it now, Mel," he insisted before she could object.

"All right."

"That's my girl."

Aaron briefly wondered how the truck had driven past the ranch house without being observed. They must have entered the ranch from a side road.

"I'll call you on my way there." His voice cracked, and he quickly cleared his throat to cover it. "Keep your phone with you at all times."

He hoped she'd say something about missing him or wanting him to stay safe before hanging up. She didn't.

"Where are you off to?" Nancy called after him as he headed for the door. "Your dinner's ready."

"There's a possible horse theft in progress at The Small Change."

He said no more. Nancy wouldn't have heard him anyway for he was halfway out the door.

Protocol may or may not have warranted him turning on the siren and breaking every speed law on the way to the ranch. After radioing the station and requesting backup, he dialed Shonda and Eduardo. Despite being off duty, they both promised to be ready within minutes. Because Eduardo was more familiar with the towns-folk, Aaron ordered him to track down Theo McGraw, the owner of The Small Change, or Theo's daughter. And of course, Cara Dempsey, manager of the mustang sanctuary. He told Eduardo to have her meet him at the gate leading to the pastures in order to unlock it.

Lastly, he instructed Eduardo to very clearly warn Josh Dempsey, Cara's notoriously hot-headed husband, to stay away. This was police business; they didn't need civilians interfering. Well-intentioned or not.

When he finished, he called Mel again. She didn't answer and after five rings, her voice-mail greeting sounded. Swearing, and accelerating on the open road, he tried again. Still no answer. He'd have thrown the phone onto the floor in frustration, but he needed it handy in case she called him back.

Was her battery dead or had something happened to her? Pounding a fist on the steering wheel, he turned sharply onto the dirt road leading to The Small Change. The SUV's wheels sprayed a shower of dirt into the air.

What a fool he'd been to let her go. He should have run after her at the inn, refusing to take no for an answer. Convince her he truly wanted to marry her, not just fulfill an obligation. Swept her off her feet. Treated her the way she deserved to be treated. Wooed her and charmed her and demonstrated through words and actions that they were meant to be together. That she was the one he'd been waiting for. The one who mattered more than anyone else.

Would she have believed him? Aaron vowed he'd move heaven and earth to show her when this was all over and prayed he had the chance.

Flying past the ranch house, he silenced his siren and drove to the horse stables. Mel's truck was there. Dark. Still. Empty. As badly as he wanted to catch the horse thieves, he wouldn't move onward without making sure she was safe. His SUV idling, he hopped out and jogged toward her truck.

Mel's head popped up before he reached the

driver's door, and she lowered her window. "I'm okay."

He stood there long enough to catch his breath and whisper a soft, "Thank you."

She opened the door.

"You're not coming with me," he barked, correctly reading her intent.

"I could—"

"No way."

"Then hurry, Aaron. Catch the bad guys."

He turned to go. At the last second, he changed his mind. Caressing her cheek through the open window, he said, "Wait for me. I'll be back."

"Be careful," was all she said.

MAYBE AARON SHOULD have brought Mel along after all. No sooner was he driving behind the outbuildings than he realized he had no clue where the gate to the pastures was located. Almost immediately, a pair of zigzagging headlights came toward him. Suspecting it was Cara Dempsey, he slowed to a stop.

She motioned for him to follow, and Aaron

noticed she had a passenger. Her husband, Josh.
They apparently hadn't heeded Eduardo's warning for Josh to stay away.

At the end of the corral, Cara stopped. She and
Josh both exited the Jeep. By the time Aaron
neared, Josh was inserting a key into the padlock.

"Don't think you're going after them by yourself," the tall, lanky man said.

Aaron figured there was no sense fighting
him. "Cara stays behind. If not, I'll arrest you
both for interfering with an investigation."

"Got it."

The padlock released, and the chain securing
the gate fell away. Josh swung open the gate just
as Cara came around to grab it, her long black
hair swinging in the breeze. Josh had probably
tasked her with shutting the gate behind them.

"If you don't hear from us in the next twenty
minutes," Aaron told her, "call the sheriff's office in Rio Verde." He passed her a card.

"Will do." She looked worried and not at all
happy her husband was going with Aaron.

The two men jumped into Aaron's SUV and took off. Josh gave directions, his voice clipped. By now, darkness had fallen. Aaron phoned Eduardo and Shonda for updates as he navigated the narrow, winding dirt road. Eduardo reported that Theo McGraw was in the hospital after a bad fall, and his family was at his side.

"These guys are either incredibly brave or incredibly stupid," Josh said. "Attempting a second theft at the same ranch they hit last time."

"They probably learned the McGraws weren't home." Another reason to believe the thieves had access to inside information.

Landscape, illuminated by moonlight, flew by as they traveled the two miles to the sanctuary. Aaron grew impatient when their progress was impeded by having to stop and unlock two more gates separating the cattle grazing sections from the sanctuary. Josh indicated a knocked-over post and tangled barbed wire while unlocking the third gate. "They cut the fences. There's going to be chaos tomorrow."

Escaping cattle was a problem. It was also the least of Aaron's concerns.

Over the next rise, the sanctuary appeared.

Aaron instantly spotted the barely visible outline of a truck and trailer parked along the fence. He'd cut his headlights a mile back to avoid detection. Now, he slowed his speed, hoping the thieves didn't see them until it was too late.

Luck, unfortunately, wasn't on their side. All at once, the thieves executed a one-eighty and pulled away, the truck tires spinning. They, too, had cut their headlights.

"Dammit," Aaron grumbled and went after them, hitting the gas and going as fast as he dared.

To Josh he said, "Did they get any horses?"

"I can't tell."

Hauling the trailer, even empty, slowed the thieves enough that Aaron was able to catch up. According to the last transmission on the radio, Eduardo, Shonda and three backup units from the Scottsdale Police Department were en route with an ETA of five minutes.

"Don't let them get away," Josh said, pounding his closed fist on the dash.

"I'm trying."

The driver of the truck was obviously no stranger to these hills.

"Where does this road lead?" Aaron asked.

"To the north, it connects with a county maintenance road," Josh said. He'd been making phone calls to Theo McGraw's family and Ray Hartman, putting them on the alert about the loose cattle. "To the south, it dead-ends at the base of the mountain."

Aaron radioed in the information, stating that he and his approaching backup should attempt to force the thieves toward the mountain. He then flipped on his siren and flashing lights.

In the distance, he spotted a fast-moving storm of white, red and blue lights from what had to be at least five emergency vehicles. A helicopter suddenly materialized from behind the mountain, its spotlight cutting a path across ground below.

The cavalry had officially arrived.

Attempting to escape, the truck and trailer veered off the dirt road, bouncing wildly over the rough terrain. Aaron and the emergency vehicles changed course.

Big mistake on the thieves' part. Traveling too fast, they hit a ditch and lost control.

The truck tilted high on its two right wheels and hung suspended in midair for several precarious heartbeats. Only the weight of the trailer prevented it from rolling. Coming down hard, the truck made a loud crashing sound, then sat, heaving and groaning like a wounded animal.

Within seconds, the thieves were surrounded on all sides by six vehicles, including Aaron's, and above by the helicopter. Two more emergency vehicles could be seen in the distance, one of them Shonda's.

Aaron grabbed his transmitter and activated the loudspeaker. "This is the Maricopa County Sheriff's Department. Remain where you are." He then reached for where his rifle was stored. No telling if these men were armed or what they might do.

He stared hard at Josh, rifle in hand. "Do not get out of this vehicle under any circumstances."

The other man's jaw visibly clenched, but he stayed put.

Taking the suspects into custody was almost anticlimactic. The pair emerged from their vehicle, arms in the air, averting their gazes from the blinding glare of numerous flashlights and headlights. The helicopter's spotlight was trained on them as well.

Aaron and Eduardo quickly subdued and cuffed them. Both were belligerent when Aaron recited their rights. Both refused to give any information, with the taller one swearing profusely and telling the shorter one to, "Shut your mouth," as they were separated and loaded into the backs of police vehicles for the drive to Scottsdale.

It was only then that Aaron recognized the taller man. He'd seen him in the feed store not two hours earlier, standing at the counter, chatting up the assistant manager.

Bells went off in Aaron's head. The feed store!

It was a place where horse folk gathered and conversed, where announcements were posted on the bulletin board and where supplies were purchased and questions asked of the staff.

It was a place where someone intent on stealing horses might obtain all the information necessary to carry out their thefts. Especially if they had an accomplice, either a knowing or unknowing one.

By now, the two remaining vehicles had showed up. A half dozen uniformed law-enforcement officers surrounded the truck. Two more were searching the empty trailer. The sound of voices combined with radio transmissions and the choppy hum of the exiting helicopter to create a noisy din. Whatever horses had been in the area were long gone, retreating to an out of sight corner of the sanctuary.

"Eduardo." Aaron hailed his fellow deputy. "I'm leaving. You're in charge."

"Where are you going?"

"Following up a lead. And I need to hurry before word of this spreads."

"Got it."

Cara was still waiting at the first gate when Aaron dropped off Josh. Fully intending to track down the assistant manager, he took a few minutes to stop at the horse stables.

Mel wasn't in her truck where he'd told her to remain. Figured. He found her in the horse stall with the foal, bent over her small patient. Also figured.

"You aren't good at following orders."

She glanced up at him. "I saw the helicopter leaving and assumed the coast was clear."

"He doing any better?" Aaron moved toward the stall.

"Not at all." Sadness filled her voice. "It's been one thing after another with this poor little guy. I'm completely out of options. It's up to him now. He either decides to fight and live, or he gives up."

Aaron didn't have to be an expert to see the foal was at death's door. His eyes were listless, his coat dull, his ribs protruded and he hung his head low as if it were too heavy for his neck.

"I'm sorry to hear that."

"I take it you caught the bad guys?" Mel asked.

"They're being transported now and should spend at least one night in jail, courtesy of the county, before being arraigned."

"I'm glad."

She looked up from the foal and for the first time that night, smiled. "You did good, Aaron."

He stared at her, struck utterly speechless. Her worry over the foal accentuated her features and gave her a soft, glowing beauty. Aaron was enamored. Captivated. Charmed. In love.

The realization stunned him. He *was* in love with Mel and had been for some time.

She met his gaze, and the spark he often sensed between them crackled. She must feel the same. What else could account for the longing in her eyes?

The radio attached to his collar went off, reminding him that duty called. "I have to leave." Tear himself away was more accurate. "I'm following up on a lead."

"Okay. Be careful." When he didn't move, she asked, "Something wrong?"

Nothing he could tell her. Not right now. Later, if all went well.

"Do you happen to know the name of the assistant manager at the feed store?"

"It's Gail. Why?"

"She may have a connection to the horse thefts."

Mel gasped softly. "I don't believe it. She's always been so nice and helpful to me."

"I'm not saying she's involved, Only that she may know something useful to the investigation. I saw her and one of the thieves talking at the store earlier." Aaron took out the small pad and pen he always carried. "What's her last name?"

"Saunders. Her uncle owns the store. I have his number if you need it."

"That would help. Yes."

"I also know where she lives. It's not far from my house."

"Can you give me the address?"

"I'll do better than that. I'll show you."

"Not a chance, Mel. This is official business."

"And I'm someone with information who can assist with a case that's very important to me. To this whole town."

"I get that. But I'm not changing my mind."

She reluctantly relented and recited the address.

Radioing Shonda, Aaron instructed the rookie deputy to meet him at Gail's house. While he didn't anticipate trouble, it was always better to have backup.

"Go home and get some sleep," he told Mel when he was done.

"I will. In a while. I don't want to leave Cracker Jack alone."

"Cracker Jack?"

"He needed a name."

Because Mel didn't want the foal to die without one.

"I'll come back to check on you when I'm done," he said.

"You don't have to, Aaron." She hugged the foal's neck and then straightened.

Seeing the sorrow in her eyes, he wanted to kiss her. And would have if he thought she'd welcome it.

"Yes, I do," he said. If only to tell her how he felt.

Leaving her was hard and required all his willpower. But from the moment he walked out of the stables, his entire attention became focused on his job.

Approaching Gail's house, he noted the lights were on, which Aaron hoped meant she was home. A call to Shonda confirmed she was two minutes away. He parked along the curb and waited for her.

The moment Gail answered the door and saw him and Shonda, she burst into sobs. "Oh, God. I'm sorry. It's not my fault. I was played."

All right. Not just a source of information. She was involved.

"Ms. Saunders," Aaron said, "I'm going to need you to come with me to the station for questioning in connection with a series of horse thefts in the area."

"Am I under arrest?" she squeaked.

"No, ma'am." *Not yet.*

After more tears, she went in search of her purse and to make sure the cat had food, Aaron and Shonda accompanying her. She didn't ask to take her own vehicle. Rather she agreed to let Aaron drive her, which he hoped signaled her willingness to cooperate.

Aaron left her in the back seat to confer with Shonda and instruct her to follow him and Gail to the station.

The other deputy sighed. "I would have never pegged her as the type to associate with criminals. I feel strangely let down."

"Probably why she was able to pull it off. The least likely suspect."

Gail didn't say much during the fifteen-mile trip to the nearest Sheriff's office. Aaron anticipated pulling an all-nighter and phoned Nancy to let her know. She didn't sound as mad as she usually did. Perhaps they were making progress.

Four hours later, the chief deputy released him. Gail had confessed, even telling them where in the mountains the horse thieves had constructed a makeshift horse camp.

Aaron drove straight to the horse stables at The Small Change. Mel's truck wasn't there. No surprise. It was the middle of the night, and she'd no doubt gone home for some much-needed sleep.

That didn't stop the insecurities from assailing him. Weeks—if not months—late, he'd finally admitted to loving Mel. Only she was nowhere around to hear his declaration, and, at this hour, he didn't dare call or go beating on her front door.

He may well have lost her, and it would serve him right. Aaron had only himself to blame.

Chapter Fourteen

Mel had been with Cracker Jack since 5:00 a.m.—two long, grueling hours ago. Ronnie had offered to call and reschedule all her appointments for the day, freeing up Mel to tend the foal.

On the outside, she maintained her composure. Inside, she was a wreck. The steps she'd taken were merely prolonging the inevitable. Cracker Jack had another day at the most. Possibly less.

"Please, please, sweetheart," she cooed, and scratched the foal between his ears. "Don't quit on me. If you would just try to stand."

Lying hastened his organs shutting down. Mel had already seen the beginning signs.

He did no more than slowly blink his unfocused eyes.

Within the last hour, his breathing had become labored, exhibiting an ominous, gravelly quality. Intravenously replacing the fluids lost due to his intestinal infection made no difference. The most Mel could—and possibly should—do was make him comfortable.

The giant lump lodged in her throat burned as if she'd swallowed a hot stone. This was highly unusual for her. Sure, she'd wept before when a patient didn't survive. Mel wasn't unfeeling. This time, her despair knew no bounds.

She could fault pregnancy hormones, but to blame them entirely would be a lie. Mel suffered because she hadn't healed from losing Aaron. She might never heal. Then what? Find a new line of work?

"You look plumb tuckered out."

"Hi, Dad." Mel pushed to her feet from where she knelt beside the foal, her bones aching and ready to snap in two. She didn't bother trying to smile.

"You're here early. Pull an all-nighter?"

"I went home around midnight."

"And returned at five, I was told."

"This is an emergency."

"Mel, you have to take care of yourself. Think of the baby."

"I'm planning on napping in the bunkhouse later, if no one minds."

"You really should go home. Wearing yourself out won't save that foal. Nature's going to take its course regardless of what anyone does."

Mel bent and retrieved the thermos of coffee resting in the open medical case. "Want some? It's just decaf but at least it's hot."

"Decaf's great. Dolores has me cutting back to one cup of regular coffee a day." He gave his head a dejected shake. "She's torturing me."

"She loves you."

"For no good reason I can fathom. Did Samantha tell you she entered the Richland County

Fair Rodeo next week? Theo's giving me a couple days off."

"No, and good for her."

Mel's youngest sister now had two wins under her belt, a first and a third place. She'd stopped helping Mel as much, focusing on training with Ronnie and babysitting Frankie's girls. Mel was happy for the teenager, though she'd have to find someone else to assist her. Or cut back on her practice—the least favorable option, as far as she was concerned.

Aaron wouldn't agree. He'd been nagging her a lot recently about working less. She supposed she should be glad they were talking and that he cared enough to nag. She might have to break down and hire part-time help to quiet him.

She stretched and rubbed the small of her back. "Been a long twenty-four hours."

"Heard you helped with rounding up those good-for-nothing horse thieves," her father said. "Lots of happy people today."

"They're not convicted yet."

"They will be. Caught red-handed from what Josh says."

"I'm just glad it's over." No more foals left motherless.

"How's Aaron?" Her father glanced around. "Thought he might be here."

So had Mel. "In bed, probably. He had a longer night than any of us."

What would it be like waking up next to him? They'd never experienced that and likely wouldn't. For a moment before he left to talk to Gail, Mel had sensed a change in him and hope flared—only to have it extinguished.

Why was it she and Aaron seemed destined to always be on the wrong track at different times? Now, permanently.

"It's a shame things didn't work out between you and him," her father said. "He's a good man."

"Guess it wasn't meant to be."

"Don't reckon you'd patch things up, given the chance?"

Yes.

"I'm not sure that's what he wants." Mel glanced down at Cracker Jack. There had been no change in the last five minutes.

"Nancy's coming to dinner this week. You mind?"

Her father's offhand remark got her attention. "No. Why would I?"

"Could be awkward."

"She and Dolores are friends."

"Nancy knows about the baby. She mentioned it when she and Dolores were on the phone last night."

So, Aaron had finally told her. "Really."

"Dolores said she acted like she didn't mind. But here's the interesting part. She mentioned a duplex apartment one of their Bunko ladies has for rent."

"Oh." That surprised Mel.

Was Nancy moving out to give Aaron space for when the baby came or because they'd fought over Mel? She was curious, though uncertain if she should ask.

The foal suddenly made a pathetic wuffling

sound. Mel bent and petted his neck, noting his hide was losing its elasticity.

"I wish there was more I could do."

"Have you tried giving him honey?" her father asked.

"Yes. Twice." Mel didn't usually subscribe to home remedies. This time, however, she'd been desperate.

"What about salt? They say if you rub the inside of a foal's mouth with salt, it'll make him thirsty and encourage him to drink."

Mel studied Cracker Jack. He was lying on his side in the soft sawdust bedding. She looked closer to make sure his narrow chest was expanding and contracting. "I'm not sure he's strong enough to drink anymore."

"Might be time to let him go."

She knew her father was right; she just didn't have the willpower to walk away. Mel vowed if he started to suffer, she would make the difficult decision all vets dreaded.

"How did Theo take the news of the horse

thieves' capture?" Small talk kept her spirits from sinking any lower.

"Blames himself for not being here."

The Small Change owner was still in the hospital, receiving treatment for his fall, though he was expected to be released before the coming weekend.

"That's ridiculous," Mel said.

"Of course it is."

"You talk to Gail's uncle? How's he doing?"

"He's devastated, naturally. Can't believe she betrayed him and the ranchers. He'd have sold the store years ago if not for her. She's his right hand. Or was. Almost like a daughter to him."

"I can't imagine what he's feeling."

Then again, maybe she could. A little, anyway. Mel had felt betrayed when she learned about Samantha and Carrie Anne. Eventually, she'd come to understand and forgive her father. She had Aaron to thank for that valuable lesson.

Seems one good thing had come out of their relationship. Two, counting the baby.

Her father started to speak, only to pause. His

cell phone must've been on vibrate for he removed it from his pocket and answered with a robust, "Ray Hartman speaking."

She watched his expression change by degrees as he listened, going from interest to shock to excitement.

"Right," he said, grinning broadly. "Be there as soon as I can."

"What's going on?" Mel asked.

"The horse thieves had a makeshift holding camp on the east side of the mountain, about a mile from Javelina Crossing. Gail told the authorities all about it."

"I know. Aaron left me a text message."

According to Gail, when the thieves stole enough horses to fill a stock trailer, they would transport them to a slaughterhouse across the state line that didn't ask a lot of questions. Mel was appalled. She was also shocked that someone she dealt with on a regular basis and had liked was involved.

"Well, believe it or not," her dad said, "Game

and Fish rangers were able to locate the holding camp. Five horses are there."

The number screamed at Mel. "Five?"

"All mares. Could be they're the pregnant ones stolen from the maternity pasture."

Cracker Jack's dam might be among them!

"The rangers are sending me directions. I'm headed out there now with a truck and trailer."

Mel scrambled to collect her equipment. "I'm coming with you!"

"'Fraid not, honey."

"The mares might require medical attention," she insisted.

"Which you'll give them the moment I return. But, for now, you're needed here." He entered the stall and took her by the shoulders. "You keep that foal alive for a couple more hours. You hear me?"

His words fired Mel's determination. She could do it. She could keep Cracker Jack alive. She refused to entertain the thought of anything else.

"Hurry, Dad."

He left, and Mel wasted no time tending to her patient. The wait was excruciating. Thirty minutes later, Samantha unexpectedly showed up.

"Can I help?" she asked.

"I thought you were babysitting."

"Nancy's watching the girls."

Would wonders never cease?

Mel gave her sister a look. "Did Dad send you?"

"He called and told me what happened. Coming here was my idea."

The teenager's sincerity touched Mel, making refusing her impossible. Besides, she'd recently grown fond of having her youngest sibling tagging along.

"You don't by chance have a box of salt," she asked.

Samantha looked at her strangely. "Salt?"

"It's Dad's idea. Run to the ranch house and ask whoever's there if we can borrow some. I think I saw the housekeeper's car pull in a little while ago."

Mel and Samantha kept up a constant conversation with Cracker Jack, assuring him that his mother was on her way, even though Mel didn't know for sure. Calls to her father went straight to voice mail, but that was expected, considering he was at the base of the mountain.

Finally, at long last, Mel heard the rumble and clang of a heavily loaded livestock trailer. Samantha ran down the aisle, returning moments later to report the good news.

"It's them! They're here."

Mel bent and, cradling Cracker Jack's small head between her hands, she kissed his warm nose. "Stay with us, sweetheart."

As if he understood, the foal opened his eyes and blew out a weak breath that felt like the brush of dandelion fluff on Mel's face.

She couldn't wait. Together, she and Samantha left the stall and went out to where her father had parked the truck and trailer in front of the stables. The doors of the truck flew open and several ranch hands spilled out, along with her father.

That wasn't what had Mel's undivided attention, however. She stared at the SUV with the official logo on the side parked behind the trailer. The one with the driver behind the steering wheel wearing a familiar dark Stetson and aviator sunglasses.

AARON WAS HALFWAY out of the SUV when Mel reached him. Her riotously pounding heart made speaking difficult, and she needed a moment to recover.

"Wh-what are you doing here?" she managed.

"I went with the Game and Fish rangers to retrieve the horses. They're considered live evidence and will be held in a secure facility until the trial is finished, if there is a trial."

"Did the thieves confess?"

"No. I wouldn't be surprised if they eventually accepted a plea agreement. Gail's statement is pretty damning."

"Will she get in trouble?" Mel was thinking of the feed store owner.

"Her confession and willingness to testify will go a long way in reducing her charges."

"I still can't believe she was involved."

"According to her, she wasn't in on it from the beginning. She genuinely believed Monty Schartz—he's one of the two perpetrators—was romantically interested in her and that his questions about her job and the goings-on in town were because he cared."

In her early forties, living alone, divorced for over fifteen years, no children. It was easy for Mel to see how Gail might have been taken advantage of by a man pretending to like her.

"Eventually," Aaron said, "she figured out what was going on."

"Why didn't she turn this Monty and his partner in?"

"She claimed by then she was afraid of him and what he might do to her."

"Poor Gail. She must have felt vulnerable and in over her head."

Aaron had been in deputy mode since arriving. Now, his expression softened around the edges as he met her gaze. "I can't say much more. This is a pending investigation."

"I understand." Throwing caution to the wind, she touched his arm. "You must be exhausted."

Lines of tension marred his handsome face, and weariness showed in his eyes when he removed his aviators.

For a long minute, they simply stood there. Mel willed him to say the words she yearned to hear. The ones that would erase all her doubts and allow her to reveal what was in her heart.

"Mel. I—"

He was cut off when one of the ranch hands lowered the rear gate on the trailer with a metallic bang. Inside the trailer, the restless horses stomped and shifted and kicked. The nearest one lifted her head high and whinnied shrilly. In the enclosed space, the sound was deafening.

Samantha hopped onto the trailer's running board and peeked inside. Ignoring their father's warning to be careful, she reached her arm through the opening and petted one of the mares.

"I'd better help with the unloading," Mel said.

"Right." Aaron put on his sunglasses and returned to his SUV. Standing by the open driver's door, he spoke into his radio.

Mel sighed, wishing she knew what he'd been about to say to her.

The first mare backed out of the large trailer and down the ramp, spinning around the instant her hooves made contact with the ground. A ranch hand grabbed hold of her lead rope before she could get away.

Mel quickly assessed the mare. She wasn't Cracker Jack's dam. And other than a few nicks and cuts and a thick layer of dirt, she appeared to be in good shape. The ranch hand led her off to the maternity corral for a long drink of water and all the hay she could eat.

The next three mares looked much the same and were equally excited to be home. By the time the last mare was unloaded, Mel was at her wit's end. But with a shiny copper coat, four matching white stockings and a rounded udder hanging low, there was little doubt Cracker Jack and his mama were about to be reunited.

Jerking hard on the lead rope, the mare gave Mel's father a difficult time.

"I'll take her, Dad."

"You sure? She's a handful."

"She's just looking for her baby."

He passed her the lead rope. "I'll be by once we get these other girls settled in. Cara's already waiting. Called me three times."

Mel started walking toward the stables. As she rounded the corner, she glanced back to see her father shaking hands with Aaron. He must be thanking Aaron for the help. At the last second, they broke into laughter. When had they become so chummy?

The impatient mare practically dragged Mel along as they entered the stables.

"I know." Mel held the mare to a walk when she would've trotted ahead. "I'm in a rush, too."

"Mind if I come?"

Hearing Aaron's voice behind her had Mel stopping in her tracks, much to the mare's consternation. Mel had expected him to leave, but he hadn't. Instead, he'd come after her. Ran, apparently. She warned herself not to make more of this than there was.

"Wouldn't you rather go home?" she asked. "Kaylee must be waiting."

"What, and miss the big reunion?" He caught up with her, and together with the mare they started for the stall.

She shoved her disappointment aside. He'd been concerned about the foal. Not her.

As they neared the stall, Mel fervently hoped the mare hadn't been returned only to see her baby die. She must have suddenly smelled the foal for she broke free of Mel's grip and charged ahead the last twenty feet, ramming her large, broad body into the stall door. Nickering loudly, she pranced in place and anxiously bobbed her head.

Mel and Aaron hurried. Hearing a feeble greeting from inside the stall, she nearly let out a sigh. Cracker Jack was still alive and recognized his mama.

"Be careful," Aaron warned when Mel squeezed in front of the mare.

Opening the stall door, she tripped while getting out of the way before the mare rushed in, whinnying more softly now. Stopping in front of Cracker Jack, she lowered her head and sniffed him. He tried to rise, only his weak legs refused to support him.

"Are you okay?" Aaron pulled Mel aside, though she was no longer in any danger.

"Fine." She'd bumped her elbow on the stall door but hardly noticed the slight sting. She was too worried about Cracker Jack.

Concern flashed in Aaron's eyes, and he held her arm. "What about the baby?"

"Really, I'm fine. I just lost my balance for a second."

"You should get checked out by a doctor."

"And you're overreacting."

"I'm insisting. Visit the clinic at least," he said. "I'll go with you."

He was being ridiculous. And adorable. She considered visiting the clinic if only to spend more time with him.

Cracker Jack suddenly positioned his front

feet beneath him and struggled to rise. Falling back with a grunt, he blew out an exhausted breath. His mother nudged him with her warm nose.

"He can't stand without help." Breaking away from Aaron, Mel went into the stall.

He followed her in. "Careful. She might kick or bite you."

It was good advice. The mare's instincts were to protect her baby. Help could be perceived as a threat.

Aaron's concerns turned out to be unfounded. The mare allowed Mel to lift Cracker Jack to a standing position. With Aaron supporting the foal's hind end, she pushed his nose toward his mama's udder and waited.

Despite being separated for several weeks, the mare still had milk, though it might take several days for her to produce enough to meet Cracker Jack's needs.

Unfortunately, he was too weak to latch on, try as he might.

"Come on, sweetheart," Mel coaxed.

"What if he won't eat?" Aaron asked.

Mel continued nudging Cracker Jack. "Then I'll see if he'll drink from a bucket or bottle. Now that he's with his mama, there's a chance he'll fight. He's already more alert and responsive."

The mare swung her large head around and nuzzled Cracker Jack, ignoring Aaron. The next moment, the foal summoned all his strength and finally latched on.

"He's nursing!" Mel exclaimed.

Aaron grinned. "Well, I'll be."

Cracker Jack let go a couple minutes later. Completely depleted, he lay back down, his mama standing guard. Mel didn't complain. Emotional nourishment was just as important as physical nourishment.

She quickly poured what manufactured mare's milk remained from earlier into a shallow pan and set it under Cracker Jack's nose. He drank about a cup. Not much, but more than Mel could have dreamed possible two hours ago. She'd try again once the foal had rested.

"You're crying," Aaron said softly.

"Am I?" She wiped at her cheeks with the back of her hand.

He came over to her. Tilting her chin up, he brushed away her tears with the pad of his thumb. "He's going to be all right."

"He still has a long road ahead, but I think he'll make it."

"Like us." Aaron's eyes roved over her face as if drinking in every detail.

"Aaron..."

He didn't let her finish. Drawing her into the aisle, he pulled her close. "When I was here last night, watching you with the foal, I realized something." He lowered his head until his mouth was inches from hers. "Something important."

"What?" Her pulse beat faster.

"I love you, Mel."

"You do?" She wanted to throw herself into his arms, but she resisted, requiring more from him than a declaration. "What changed your mind?"

"I'm pretty sure I've been falling for you since the moment we met. I was just too stupid to admit it. And too scared."

"Of Nancy?"

"Hardly." He laughed. "She's indomitable, but I'm tougher." He put an arm around her waist, anchoring her to him. "I was afraid that what I was feeling was fleeting. Or that you couldn't possibly love me in return."

"You're right." The wall she'd erected around her heart to shield herself from hurt crumbled to pieces. "You are stupid."

"Trust me." He brushed his lips across hers. "I've smartened up considerably in the last day. The next time I propose, I'll do such an incredible job, there's no way you'll say no."

"Next time?"

"I want to marry you, Mel. Not because it's the right thing for our baby, though it is, but because I love you and can't stand the thought of not spending every day for the rest of my life with you."

She very much liked the sound of that.

He kissed her then, delicately and tenderly. "First, however, we date. Then, after we've gotten to know each other, we'll get ready for the baby."

"You don't say?"

He'd suggested dating before, but Mel hadn't been ready. The last two miserable weeks had her reconsidering. The last few minutes had her changing her mind completely.

She mustered her courage and stared into his eyes. There, shining bright and true, was the love she'd been wanting and waiting for her whole life.

"I love you, too." There, she'd said it.

"Are you free tonight?"

She smiled, joy filling her to bursting. "Are you asking me out?"

"I'm starting with asking you out. I may work up to more as the night goes on. Keep in mind, I still have a ring."

Mel didn't hesitate. "Yes, I'm free." And she'd say yes to anything else he suggested.

His lips met hers then, making silent promises for tonight and the wonderful, beautiful future in store for them. Whatever problems they faced, and there were many, Mel was confident she and Aaron would overcome them. They were a family now—Mel, Aaron, Kaylee and the baby.

How silly Mel had been to resist a committed relationship. As she and Aaron kissed and kissed, unable to get enough of each other, Mel couldn't imagine anything better than joining her life with his, forever and ever.

* * * * *

MILLS & BOON®
Large Print – April 2017

ROMANCE

A Di Sione for the Greek's Pleasure	Kate Hewitt
The Prince's Pregnant Mistress	Maisey Yates
The Greek's Christmas Bride	Lynne Graham
The Guardian's Virgin Ward	Caitlin Crews
A Royal Vow of Convenience	Sharon Kendrick
The Desert King's Secret Heir	Annie West
Married for the Sheikh's Duty	Tara Pammi
Winter Wedding for the Prince	Barbara Wallace
Christmas in the Boss's Castle	Scarlet Wilson
Her Festive Doorstep Baby	Kate Hardy
Holiday with the Mystery Italian	Ellie Darkins

HISTORICAL

Bound by a Scandalous Secret	Diane Gaston
The Governess's Secret Baby	Janice Preston
Married for His Convenience	Eleanor Webster
The Saxon Outlaw's Revenge	Elisabeth Hobbes
In Debt to the Enemy Lord	Nicole Locke

MEDICAL

Waking Up to Dr Gorgeous	Emily Forbes
Swept Away by the Seductive Stranger	Amy Andrews
One Kiss in Tokyo...	Scarlet Wilson
The Courage to Love Her Army Doc	Karin Baine
Reawakened by the Surgeon's Touch	Jennifer Taylor
Second Chance with Lord Branscombe	Joanna Neil

0317 GEN STD LP

MILLS & BOON®
Hardback – May 2017

ROMANCE

The Sheikh's Bought Wife	Sharon Kendrick
The Innocent's Shameful Secret	Sara Craven
The Magnate's Tempestuous Marriage	Miranda Lee
The Forced Bride of Alazar	Kate Hewitt
Bound by the Sultan's Baby	Carol Marinelli
Blackmailed Down the Aisle	Louise Fuller
Di Marcello's Secret Son	Rachael Thomas
The Italian's Vengeful Seduction	Bella Frances
Conveniently Wed to the Greek	Kandy Shepherd
His Shy Cinderella	Kate Hardy
Falling for the Rebel Princess	Ellie Darkins
Claimed by the Wealthy Magnate	Nina Milne
Mummy, Nurse...Duchess?	Kate Hardy
Falling for the Foster Mum	Karin Baine
The Doctor and the Princess	Scarlet Wilson
Miracle for the Neurosurgeon	Lynne Marshall
English Rose for the Sicilian Doc	Annie Claydon
Engaged to the Doctor Sheikh	Meredith Webber
The Marriage Contract	Kat Cantrell
Triplets for the Texan	Janice Maynard

0417 GEN STD HB

MILLS & BOON®
Large Print – May 2017

ROMANCE

A Deal for the Di Sione Ring	Jennifer Hayward
The Italian's Pregnant Virgin	Maisey Yates
A Dangerous Taste of Passion	Anne Mather
Bought to Carry His Heir	Jane Porter
Married for the Greek's Convenience	Michelle Smart
Bound by His Desert Diamond	Andie Brock
A Child Claimed by Gold	Rachael Thomas
Her New Year Baby Secret	Jessica Gilmore
Slow Dance with the Best Man	Sophie Pembroke
The Prince's Convenient Proposal	Barbara Hannay
The Tycoon's Reluctant Cinderella	Therese Beharrie

HISTORICAL

The Wedding Game	Christine Merrill
Secrets of the Marriage Bed	Ann Lethbridge
Compromising the Duke's Daughter	Mary Brendan
In Bed with the Viking Warrior	Harper St. George
Married to Her Enemy	Jenni Fletcher

MEDICAL

The Nurse's Christmas Gift	Tina Beckett
The Midwife's Pregnancy Miracle	Kate Hardy
Their First Family Christmas	Alison Roberts
The Nightshift Before Christmas	Annie O'Neil
It Started at Christmas...	Janice Lynn
Unwrapped by the Duke	Amy Ruttan

0417 GEN STD LP

MILLS & BOON®

Why shop at millsandboon.co.uk?

Each year, thousands of romance readers find their perfect read at millsandboon.co.uk. That's because we're passionate about bringing you the very best romantic fiction. Here are some of the advantages of shopping at www.millsandboon.co.uk:

* **Get new books first**—you'll be able to buy your favourite books one month before they hit the shops

* **Get exclusive discounts**—you'll also be able to buy our specially created monthly collections, with up to 50% off the RRP

* **Find your favourite authors**—latest news, interviews and new releases for all your favourite authors and series on our website, plus ideas for what to try next

* **Join in**—once you've bought your favourite books, don't forget to register with us to rate, review and join in the discussions

Visit **www.millsandboon.co.uk**
for all this and more today!